Bolan took ou
with deadly accuracy

When the commander of the rapidly shrinking fleet realized the number of hits they were taking, the boats roared toward the open sea.

"Let's move out," the Executioner shouted, "before they figure out where to make a landing and come after us."

"What about you?"

"I'll stay here awhile longer to convince them it's a bad idea to come ashore."

Seward hesitated, then gave the warrior a look that said he felt responsible for leading them into the ambush. "We're not leaving without you."

"The hell you aren't. If I'm not there when you ship out, just leave one of the boats behind. Don't worry about me. I didn't come all this way just to die on you."

Seward nodded, then he and his lieutenant shouldered their wounded comrade and hurried through the brush.

Bolan stayed behind, hoping to buy some time for the remnants of the strike force.

MACK BOLAN.
The Executioner

DON PENDLETON'S
THE EXECUTIONER®
FEATURING MACK BOLAN®

MAXIMUM IMPACT

A GOLD EAGLE BOOK FROM
WORLDWIDE.

TORONTO • NEW YORK • LONDON
AMSTERDAM • PARIS • SYDNEY • HAMBURG
STOCKHOLM • ATHENS • TOKYO • MILAN
MADRID • WARSAW • BUDAPEST • AUCKLAND

First edition December 1994

ISBN 0-373-61192-7

Special thanks and acknowledgment to
Rich Rainey for his contribution to this work.

MAXIMUM IMPACT

Printed in U.S.A.

Plots, true or false, are necessary things, to raise up commonwealths and ruin kings.

—John Dryden,
1651–1700

Those men who plot to seize what rightfully belongs to others will pay the ultimate price for their treachery.

—Mack Bolan

THE
MACK BOLAN®
LEGEND

Nothing less than a war could have fashioned the destiny of the man called Mack Bolan. Bolan earned the Executioner title in the jungle hell of Vietnam.

But this soldier also wore another name—Sergeant Mercy. He was so tagged because of the compassion he showed to wounded comrades-in-arms and Vietnamese civilians.

Mack Bolan's second tour of duty ended prematurely when he was given emergency leave to return home and bury his family, victims of the Mob. Then he declared a one-man war against the Mafia.

He confronted the Families head-on from coast to coast, and soon a hope of victory began to appear. But Bolan had broken society's every rule. That same society started gunning for this elusive warrior—to no avail.

So Bolan was offered amnesty to work within the system against terrorism. This time, as an employee of Uncle Sam, Bolan became Colonel John Phoenix. With a command center at Stony Man Farm in Virginia, he and his new allies—Able Team and Phoenix Force—waged relentless war on a new adversary: the KGB.

But when his one true love, April Rose, died at the hands of the Soviet terror machine, Bolan severed all ties with Establishment authority.

Now, after a lengthy lone-wolf struggle and much soul-searching, the Executioner has agreed to enter an ''arm's-length'' alliance with his government once more, reserving the right to pursue personal missions in his Everlasting War.

PROLOGUE

The shadow of the unmarked helicopter rippled across the barrier reef that jutted out from Cape Brethren like a fishhook cast into the Caribbean Sea.

The helicopter flew low over the capital's zigzag coastline, which was dotted with pastel-colored villas and palatial hotels. The white-sand beaches of the cape and its glittering casinos made it the number-one tourist attraction of the St. Andreas Islands, the small island chain on the southern rim of the Lesser Antilles.

Cape Brethren was also the cultural and politcal center of the islands and, to the heavily armed men in the helicopter, it was up for grabs. Someday soon the town would be theirs. It was only a matter of convincing the people that the real power on the island belonged to Carib Command.

The demonstration was about to begin.

The chopper flew in a contour pattern over rolling green highlands as it headed for the interior. Thrumming rotors cast flickering shadows on the lush green treetops of the ancient forest. Soon a sharp, slanting pinnacle appeared in the distance, spearing into the sky like a mammoth gray stone ski lift.

"Five minutes to the drop zone," the pilot announced.

The eleven men in the back of the chopper heard his voice over their miniature headsets, but few of them needed reminders of the location. Ever since the discovery of the Mayan-style ruins, they'd been keeping a close but covert watch on the archaeological team that descended upon the site.

The earthquake that had recently hit the island had sent stone tiers popping up through the ground like Mayan tombstones. The largely intact towers and temples made it a bonanza for scientists, and the priceless artifacts made it a gold mine for Carib Command.

As the droning and rumbling aircraft took them closer to their destination, the small band of soldiers mentally prepared themselves for battle. Their communication gear was top-of-the-line, as were their weapons: Heckler & Koch MP-5s, Sterling SMGs, smoke, gas and stun grenades. They were ready to go.

Gordon Parker, the fiftyish, clean-shaven crew chief, was proud of the strike team he'd forged from the ragtag band of mercs and cutthroats the cartel placed in his hands for training months earlier. They needed combat-ready units capable of holding their own against the island's military and police force.

He was the man to give them what they required.

Parker's last tour of duty had ended after serving only two years in the Island Defense Force, or IDF. He'd been discharged for negligence in the "accidental" death of a fellow officer who made the mistake of publicly accusing him of theft of matériel. Now he worked for Carib Command, the organization he used to sell arms to.

"Check your harness," Parker ordered, looking over the rows of commandos who sat on the hard metal benches bolted into the side of the cabin, "and check your weapons. We're almost there."

He savored the way his men crisply followed his orders. All except Travis Lathrop, the American. With his wild gray beard, the undisciplined rebel looked more like a mountain man than a soldier. He was the best in the lot—except for attitude. Lathrop had no time for Parker's spit-and-polish routines.

The American was popular with the other men. Too popular. He was loud, played by his own rules and was totally fearless. A natural leader. Sooner or later he'd make a move to take over the outfit, Parker thought. He'd do it step by step, nothing too obvious as he undermined Parker's position.

At the moment the guy was sitting there, shaking his head.

"Something wrong, soldier? I said check your weapon."

Lathrop looked up as if he'd just heard the command for the first time. Feigning compliance, he methodically looked over his Sterling submachine gun. "Still the same one I had when we got on, sir," he said in his mocking Southern drawl.

Parker yanked open the sliding cabin door, letting a fast-moving wall of wind rush into the cabin. "You don't like the way I run this outfit, Travis, you can get off here."

The American glanced at the violent sky rushing by and raised his eyebrows. Then, as if he were humoring a madman, he politely stated, "I think I'll check my weapon, sir."

Some of the men smiled, but under the harsh gaze of Parker most of them looked straight ahead.

It was going to be a long tour for Travis Lathrop. The former U.S. paratrooper had signed on as a hired gun up and down the Americas. He'd dealt with Parker's kind of martinet before and got in trouble every time. It was just the way he was.

The chopper banked suddenly and dropped like an angry wasp toward the ruins below.

KAREN HOLMES KNELT in the dirt in her sweat-soaked halter top and khaki shorts, scraping away with brush and trowel at the ancient rooftops of the pre-Columbian ruins.

Days spent in the high mountain sun had turned her skin a deep tan and lightened her reddish hair with streaks of blond. Despite the brutal sun she stayed at her task, just like the rest of the crew who'd been working straight through since morning.

The excavation was about to yield its secrets. The ropes and stakes marking off the sculptured peaks and towers of the ancient ruins made it look like a mountaintop garden ready for harvest.

So far, they'd found terra-cotta figurines, some gold altar pieces and stone monuments covered with Mayanlike glyphs that told the story of the people who built the jungle civilization.

Here at their feet could be proof that the Carib culture that dominated the islands was an extension of the Mayan empire.

A sudden thrumming sound drew Karen's attention. Looking up through the canopy of trees, she saw a heavy cargo helicopter circling the mountaintop. That was odd. Supplies weren't due for several days, and they weren't expecting company.

The helicopter swooped past the clearing the laborers had hacked out for a makeshift landing zone. Instead of landing in the clearing, the helicopter hovered above the treetops.

Squinting against the sun, Karen saw what seemed to be a group of soldiers standing in the open cabin. What were government troops doing at the dig site? "Oh, God," she said aloud.

Maybe there was some guerrilla activity in the area, and the army felt the two security men posted at the dig weren't enough to deal with them. A sudden shiver raced down her back.

A few others in the dig crew looked up at the helicopter, some curious, some irritated at the distraction from their work.

One of the security men, an islander in a white shirt, badge and Sam Browne gun belt, hurried past Karen and headed for the helicopter as if he knew something were wrong.

In twos and threes the rest of the group followed the man, drawn by the sound of the rotors like children following the chimes of an ice-cream truck.

A few moments later Karen headed toward the small clearing where the down-wash from the hovering craft rushed through the wildly shaking foliage.

A group of workers from the dig stood at the edge of the clearing, staring in fascination at airborne troops jumping from the helicopter. The black-clad commandos abseiled down thin nylon cords like spiders on silk strings.

As soon as they touched the soft jungle floor, they released their harness straps and stepped out of the way for the next group of soldiers to sail down.

The security guard stepped forward in confusion, shouting something to one of the soldiers nearest him.

The commando glanced at the guard, idly raised his Heckler & Koch submachine gun and shot him in the chest. Gouts of blood spouted in the air as he fell dead to the ground, hand still reaching for his holstered gun.

For one frozen moment the members of the expedition stared in horror at the slain guard.

The rest of the men touched ground, slipped off their harnesses and aimed their weapons at the panic-stricken scientists.

Ignoring the pleas and tears, they triggered a barrage at the unarmed civilians. The first volley punched a half-dozen men and women back into the trees, flesh and blood spraying wildly as they dropped to the ground. The raiders stepped forward, brutally delivering kill shots to the survivors of the first assault.

Gordon Parker strode through the rain forest, urging his men as they triggered full-auto bursts into the remaining scientists.

The bullets chewed through flesh, chopped into tree trunks and whacked into the wooden stakes that marked off the different sectors of the dig.

In the distance a handful of men and women ran for their lives. But there was nowhere to run. The black-clad assassins who'd dropped from the helicopter moved quickly through the rain forest, shooting everyone in their path.

TRAVIS LATHROP BOLTED through the commandos laying waste to the forest and clamped his fingers into Parker's shoulder, roughly spinning him. "Dammit, Parker! You gotta stop this!"

Parker glared at him, then shrugged free from his grip. "What's wrong, Travis? Lost your nerve?"

"Nerve, hell," Lathrop growled. "I signed on to fight a war, not shoot people in cold blood. You said we were coming out here to hunt down an elite Intelligence unit. These are civilians."

"*They* are the enemy," Parker shouted. "This is the first full engagement of Carib Command.

"This is a massacre, Parker. Nothing more."

"Nothing but. Either you join in, or muster out." He moved subtly so his Heckler & Koch covered Lathrop.

The American had done the same, instinctively turning his weapon on Parker. Each man was just a trigger-pull away from eternity.

Parker nodded toward the uphill site where a woman ran like a deer through the forest, jumping over fallen brush and hurtling toward safety. "She's all yours, Travis."

Lathrop set off on a slow jog through the forest. Though the girl zigged and zagged, she never strayed far from a straight line. Before long his path would intersect with hers.

He glanced behind him and saw one of Parker's commandos trailing him to make sure he carried out his task.

In the distance he heard bursts of automatic fire, followed by the death cries of men and women shot down like wild beasts.

KAREN LEAPT over a fallen tree trunk like an Olympic hurdler, then crashed through thorny brush. The fleeting pain was overwhelmed by fear of the black-clad killers who'd descended from the sky.

At the first shot she'd turned and run. She'd heard her friends cry out, heard the bullets scorching the air around her. Survival was instinctive.

The overgrown trail she was following suddenly came to an end in a green wall of vines, bamboo stalks and thin gnarled trees. End of the line. From her earlier hikes she knew that there was a drop-off beyond this section of rain forest.

Karen looked behind her and saw the silhouette of a tall man stalking forward. A moment later, when he stepped into a sunlit clearing, she could see him.

Predator and prey stared at each other for a fleeting moment. Then her stalker pushed through the rain forest like a shark parting the water.

He caught her at the edge of the drop-off where she lay in total exhaustion, her breath coming in long, shuddering gasps.

It was a good ten yards down. There were vines and snakelike roots clinging to the top, but there was no way the woman could navigate it quickly enough to get away to the next tier.

"It's no use running anymore."

"You're American!" she said, a touch of hope creeping into her voice. "What are you doing down here with these . . . murderers?"

"I'm doing what I'm told, girl." Lathrop glanced back at his Carib Command shadow, who was closing the gap. He lowered the Sterling submachine gun and tracked it across her body.

"No!" she shouted. "For God's sake—"

Lathrop pulled the trigger and the screaming stopped.

Karen fell on her back as the burst echoed over the forest. She looked up at him in shock, then at the ground beside her where slugs had burrowed into the earth. "What's going on—"

"Listen up," Lathrop growled, kneeling beside her. "Doesn't matter how, but you and me got on the wrong train. Only way out is to make you look *real* dead." In a quick blur he drew his boot knife across his forearm and smeared the blood across her shirt. "Figure you got thirty seconds to get down to that patch of jungle. Climb, jump, whatever. Just lie on your back till this is over."

"What if the others come for me?"

"Then I guess we'll both die here," he replied, lifting her as if she were weightless. He pretended to drop her off the edge, giving her a chance to get a grip before he let her go.

As she began her scuttling descent, Travis knotted his bandanna tight around his straight-line wound. Then he headed back toward the approaching commando. It was Edward Raffell, the IDF defector who used to work with Parker in the stolen-weapons racket.

"It's done," Travis said, staring him down, ready to shoot. "Now let's get the payoff."

THE VIDEOTAPE WAS running. Beneath the cover of the palm leaves and thick rain-forest undergrowth, Antonio Salvador held out his camera, covertly taping the black-clad figures desecrating the ruins. With feverish greed they smashed through the temple walls with mallets and picks inherited from Salvador's slaughtered colleagues.

Men and women he'd worked with lay in the sun, broken and bloodied like human debris. He'd be among them if he hadn't been out gathering videotape of the rain forest for his documentary about the dig. He'd come upon the scene shortly after the armed men glided down the ropes. As a precaution he'd hung back in the woods—and then the killing began. As the slaughter progressed, he moved farther and farther into the forest until he felt safe.

Now the camera in his shaky hand held testimony to a massacre.

1

The flight from Miami on the Airbus A300 wasn't crowded at all for this time of year. Hurricane season was still about a month away, which usually meant nearly all of the two hundred eighty seats would be full. On previous trips Mack Bolan, a.k.a. the Executioner, had taken to the Caribbean under civilian cover, the seats were packed with islanders returning from the U.S. and American tourists eager to soak up the good life at the hedonistic resorts that catered to their every whim.

But on this day's midmorning flight to the St. Andreas Islands, almost half of the seats were empty.

Because of the Carib Command attack on civilians working the archaeological dig, word of potential unrest on the island had reached the newspapers and news networks around the world.

While many Caribbean islands could weather the plagues of narcotraffickers and rising crime rates, the threat of open warfare on outsiders was enough to sink St. Andreas's tourist-based economy.

The increasingly belligerent and lawless Carib Command was a serious threat to islanders and incoming tourists alike. Though no one had openly taken credit for the attack at the dig, there was little doubt who was behind the massacre.

The United States had issued a travel alert to American citizens. And though many of the tourists who had planned their vacations well in advance were still visiting St. Andreas, an equal number were canceling or postponing their trips until the political situation stabilized.

That could be a long wait, Bolan thought as he looked out his window seat at the cloudless sky below.

Long stretches of blue Caribbean were broken up by sudden green-and-brown patches of land as the aircraft droned over the small island states.

Another half hour of air-conditioned flight time remained before they reached their destination.

Bolan used the time to review some of the briefing Intel provided to him about the islands.

The St. Andreas Islands were located at the southern end of the Caribbean islands collectively known as the Lesser Antilles. Like Trinidad, Grenada and Barbados, St. Andreas was relatively close to South America but still maintained its own island identity.

After centuries of Spanish, French and British rule, St. Andreas was now in its third decade of independence.

Unfortunately that sovereignty was threatened by Carib Command's network of traffickers and terrorists who masked their activities behind a patriotic front.

Bolan knew the type. He'd faced them—and fought them—all across the globe. Which was why the Justice Department's Hal Brognola had asked him to lend a hand in stabilizing the situation.

Bolan was going in solo. Brognola had assets and backup in place on the island to provide logistic support and firepower as needed, but for the most part the Executioner would be on his own.

There would be some liaison with the authorities on St. Andreas to share Intel and coordinate targets, but it would be limited to a select few.

Since many of their operations against Carib Command had been compromised by leaks and outright collaboration from within the ranks, both the Island Security Force—ISF—and the Island Defense Force had been placed under the command of one man—Colonel Jacques Mantrell.

He was the one man Bolan knew he could trust.

Mantrell was the key liaison man with the United States, the U.K. and the confederation of states in the Caribbean Regional Security System, or RSS. During the Grenada invasion and the RSS operation that reversed the coup in Trinidad, Mantrell had played a major behind-the-scenes role. Both times the colonel had provided intelligence and logistical support to Brognola and his British counterparts. There had been other, less known incidents in the Caribbean region where Mantrell had proved invaluable in maintaining the peace.

Now that Mantrell needed help in stabilizing the democratic government of St. Andreas, it was only natural that he turned to his long-standing ally.

And it was only natural that Brognola sent in the very best—the Executioner.

It would be low-key all right, Bolan thought. Before making official contact with Mantrell, the warrior wanted to study the situation for himself.

Brognola had provided him with a cover as a travel writer. The false identity was fully backstopped, complete with bylines in several different travel magazines and even a couple of travel books. His persona as a travel writer would give him a logical reason to snoop around the island.

But sooner or later Carib Command would figure out that the arrival of a travel writer and the sudden departure of several of their enforcers was more than a coincidence.

It was the simple mathematics of execution.

After scanning the briefing materials and committing them to memory, Bolan slid them back into his travel bag. The nuts-and-bolts materials would pass unnoticed through customs since they were packaged as travel articles, brochures and newspaper profiles of the key players in the St. Andreas Islands, the type of background any travel writer would be sure to have. That was the soft Intel.

The hard Intel was locked into his memory from the briefing he'd had with Brognola back in Miami, where the big Fed was doing some contingency planning for the later stages of the operation.

Bolan sank back into the comfortable first-class seat to catch a few minutes of rest before the aircraft landed at St. Andreas International Airport.

He needed it. The others on the plane were going off on vacation. The Executioner was going off to war.

2

Mack Bolan's Cape Brethren contact was expecting him at five o'clock in the afternoon.

Bolan drove into the northern side of town two hours ahead of schedule, which would give him a chance to see the sights and to see if anyone had him in *their* sights. It was a force of habit that kept him alive.

The streets of Cape Brethren were crowded with old-model American cars that moved in and out of the narrow cobblestoned roads. Their rusted surfaces had been smoothed out and repainted with thick coats of bright exterior house paint. Reconditioned Ford and Chevy sedans with big headlights and long tail fins seemed to be the most popular, with a few station wagons showing up here and there.

Then there were the new-model imports—Mercedes, Audis and Volvos. These more expensive cars belonged to cops, criminals or wealthy expatriates who'd moved to the island in the ancient days before drug dealers and the resulting decay had set in.

Bolan drove randomly through the bustling streets in the modest rental car that matched his cover as a relatively well-off tourist or professional there on business.

Island music played softly on the car radio, a mixture of steel guitar, congas, talking drums and chant-like harmonies that captured the rhythm of Carib life.

After a half hour of cruising through the winding streets, Bolan fell in with the thinning stream of traffic on the serpentine coastal road that swooped up into the hills on the southern outskirts of town.

Though the cliff-side curves were treacherous, the cars and buses picked up a near-suicidal speed until they fell into a roller-coaster cadence.

It was a good place to make someone disappear.

The Executioner traveled several miles southward before slowing at one of the pull-off areas that looked out over the sea-green Caribbean far below.

Now that he knew the lay of the land, Bolan turned around and headed back into town. He drove through the shopping district and parked in a crowded lot near the main street.

A quick walk through the outdoor stalls convinced him that the spirit of the pirates the town was named for centuries ago was still thriving. At least in the tourist shops. The locals knew better than to frequent this high-priced stretch of Cape Brethren.

Bolan killed time in a sidewalk café, reading one of the local papers until it was time for his rendezvous.

A block away from the café he turned down a wide side street that slanted downhill toward the docks. When he reached midway, Bolan climbed the steps of a brick building bearing a huge hand-lettered sign that read Island Import Chain, a distributor of American cassettes and CDs, as well as brand-name and knock-off clothes.

Just inside the entrance, one corridor led to an office and warehouse area. A second corridor opened into a small gift shop and display area, where racks of clothes and rows of cassettes and CDs were for sale to the locals.

It was almost closing time, and the shop was nearly empty. Two women and an uninterested teenager were looking through the clothes. A couple of giggling young island girls were scanning the CDs.

A man behind the counter was pretending to read the sports section of the *Brethren Beacon* while he watched Bolan with great interest.

The man looked like an American—an American who happened to be on the run. A string of tattoos detailed his career on his lean, muscled arms.

Airborne.

On his left biceps a girl's name was crossed out with a large *X*. His right biceps sported a coiled dragon.

His beard was in that stage between unshaven and unruly, and he had a wary look about him, like someone who expected the police to come looking for him for any number of reasons. He also looked like someone who could steer you to a good deal of clothes that had just fallen off the back of a truck.

The man looked at his watch, then folded his paper and dropped it loudly on the countertop. "Five o'clock," he announced. "Closing time. Please make your selections, and let a tired man get some rest."

"I don't think rest will help that attitude," one of the women said as she carried a pair of jeans to the counter.

He laughed as he rang up the sale on the cash register. "You should see me *without* my beauty sleep."

"Now, that's a frightening thought."

Bolan sauntered through the shop until the last customer left, pretending he was interested in buying something.

The man stepped out from behind the counter. Beneath the pose of the Yankee rover there was a keen intelligence at work. His eyes had the piercing quality of a man who was used to living out several covers—and seeing through others. "Like I said, it's closing time."

"Right."

"So is there anything special you're looking for?"

"Yeah," Bolan replied. "I'm looking for some gifts to bring back home."

"Something with a Caribbean flavor?"

Bolan shook his head. "More like Mediterranean," he said, finishing up the recognition phrases. He had already made a positive ID of the man from the photo and video file Brognola had shown him of the contacts they had on the island.

His name was Mark Shepard, and his import operation handled a lot more than blue jeans and blues.

"Mediterranean," Shepard mused. "We had a special order for Mediterranean products come in just a few days ago. Customer by the name of..." He looked up at Bolan for the cover name he'd been given.

"Mike Belasko."

Shepard nodded his approval. "Good. Now that we got that out of the way, welcome to the shop." He closed and locked the shop door, then pulled down the shade.

He led Bolan back to the counter and reached behind it for a small brown leather briefcase. Sliding the case across the countertop to Bolan, Shepard said, "Here's your order, Belasko. Check it out."

Bolan flipped the latches on the case and lifted the lid. Inside was an Italian-made Beretta 93-R, one of the warrior's favorite weapons.

The Beretta had served him well. With the 15-round capacity and the ability to work as a pistol or machine pistol, the 93-R covered a lot of situations.

The open case also held a folding wire stock, a sound suppressor, harness and several clips of ammunition.

Unlike Bolan's direct flight from Miami, the Beretta 93-R had taken a more roundabout journey before it was delivered to Shepard's import shop.

The warrior hefted the weapon, slapped in a clip, then set it back down on the counter.

"Feels just fine," he said.

"It's you," Shepard agreed.

Bolan studied the man who was part of Brognola's covert network in the Caribbean. The weapon did two things. It not only provided Bolan with hardware, but it established Shepard's bona fides better than any code words ever could.

"Here," Shepard said. "You'll need these, too." He handed Bolan a small read-and-rip pad with several phone numbers, addresses and names written on some of the sheets. They were contacts, safehouses and message drops that Bolan could use when the time was right—whenever things got too hot at the hotel where he'd booked himself a room under his civilian guise.

"You'll find additional weapons, comm gear, surveillance rigs and vehicles at these locations," Shepard said. "If you need anything special, go through me, not the ISF."

"Why?"

"They're getting better, but there's still too much chance of a slipup in their security. Any time ordnance or SWAT gear gets requisitioned, there are a lot of people who follow the trail."

"I thought the ISF could be trusted."

"And I thought it snowed down here before they assigned me to this station."

"What about Mantrell?"

"Mantrell is okay, and so are some of his people," Shepard replied, giving Bolan a quick rundown on members of elite ISF strike teams that he or some of the other operatives in the area had worked with successfully. "But it's the higher-ups you have to worry about."

"How high up are you talking about?"

"All the way to the top," Shepard said. "Mantrell's the key military and intelligence figure on the island. But there's a string of brigadier generals looking over his shoulder. And then you've got ministers, advisers to the prime minister. The whole schmear. A lot of these guys work both sides of the fence. In public they're fiercely loyal to the prime minister."

"In private?" Bolan suggested.

"They're sharpening knives and subtly placing them in the guy's back. These loyal supporters are the same people seen in the company of known Carib Command sponsors or underworld figures. They're bound and determined to come out on the winning side, no matter who the sinner is."

"Sounds like the politicians back home," Bolan said.

"Yeah," Shepard said. "Except some of these guys will go a lot farther at the drop of a dime. No holds barred. Theft, bribery, murder. It's a jungle."

Bolan listened carefully to Shepard's briefing on the political power brokers. There were some outright corrupt ones, some genuine supporters of the government and a lot of men who fell into the gray area in between.

"What about the Island Defense Force?" Bolan asked. "Where do they fit in? Mantrell's running both outfits, but so far you only mentioned the Island Security Force."

"Yeah. With good reason. The defense force was riddled with corruption before Mantrell took it over. He purged the ranks wherever he could, but there's still a lot of rotten apples. Death-squad types. Thieves. Guns for hire. It's an explosive situation."

"Right," Bolan said dryly. "I'm not down here to work on my tan."

Shepard suddenly paid great attention to the television set that was on a shelf behind the counter. "Looks like you might be going to work quicker than you thought."

The warrior stepped behind the counter. A thirteen-inch security monitor showed two men strolling down the street outside the import house. Two other monitors on a bottom shelf showed different angles of the street.

Shepard pressed a button, and the surveillance camera zoomed in on the men. Both looked like islanders, but one of them had a short, almost military-style haircut, and the other had long black hair parted in the middle.

They had a menacing aura about them, definitely bad news for anyone who got on their bad side.

"You notice them before?" Shepard asked.

"Couple times on the street. Figured they were trolling for a rich tourist."

"Could be," Shepard agreed. "Or maybe they're looking for someone the ISF brought to the island. They look like Carib Command to me. Can't say for sure, but I think I've seen their faces before in some of the files."

"You think I'm made already?" Bolan asked.

"Not you specifically. But I doubt it's any secret that Mantrell went through outside channels to bring in some help. Carib Command probably has all their people on the lookout."

"How secure is your operation?" Bolan asked. "Any possibility of a leak?"

"No, not from us. We're secure. But it's probably no great secret to any decent intelligence service who is operating in the area. Hell, back home we know both the friendlies and the hostile agents stationed in our territory."

Bolan knew the score. Even the allied agencies spied on one another and kept a who's who of all the players. If the ISF or IDF had Intel on some of the American operations, there was a good chance that the information made it to Carib Command.

"All right," Bolan said. "Let's say they're watching your place. They're still not sure where I fit in."

Shepard nodded as he watched the progress of the hardmen on the security monitor.

"I think it's time these two found out." The Executioner picked up the Beretta, then grabbed a denim work shirt from one of the racks and draped it over his arm.

Two minutes later he stepped out of the shop.

The two men were still there, lingering up at the corner, looking down his way. Beyond them he could see a stream of tourists passing by.

Bolan walked tentatively down the steps and glanced their way like a tourist who was worried that he'd walked into the wrong side of town.

The act worked.

Neither man bothered to hide his interest in Bolan. This was their turf, and he was their target. They laughed suddenly, their loud voices drifting to him.

Standard intimidation tactics. Get the target on edge, then get the target.

They started walking toward him.

Bolan played out his charade. After taking a few steps in their direction, he suddenly stopped as if he were now fully aware of their menacing presence. He did a quick about-face and started to walk the other way, past old warehouse buildings with shuttered metal doors and closed storefronts with painted windows and rusted padlocked doors.

They started to follow him.

At first they hung back, but as Bolan neared the end of the street that led down to the waterfront, they picked up the pace and scuffed their feet loudly on the oil-slicked street.

"Look at the man run," one of the men commented.

His partner laughed. "No way out for this one. He's ours."

"Hey, man, wait up. We want to talk to you."

Bolan ignored them as he carefully studied the landmarks that Shepard had briefed him on.

Timing was critical. He figured there was a certain grace period before they would strike—while they were figuring out if he really was the man they were seeking. Bolan wanted to maneuver them onto the battlefield of his choice.

The last thing he wanted was a firefight out in the open where innocent people might be hit or a crowd of witnesses could see him in action.

"What's the hurry, man? We're talking to you!"

Bolan glanced at his pursuers. Any doubt he had about who they worked for vanished. While the long-haired man taunted the warrior, the other one talked into a small hand-held radio with the telescopic antenna extended.

A Carib Command backup team appeared at the far end of the street, blocking Bolan's way to the waterfront.

The new arrivals stood perfectly still as they waited for the first team to herd Bolan their way.

Bolan sidestepped into the shadows at the mouth of an alley between two crumbling redbrick buildings. He strode through the debris-filled lane until he reached the spot where a section of the building jutted out and formed a small alcove.

The warrior could probably stay in the shadows and slip out the opposite end of the alley, but there would be a few critical moments when his stalkers would have a clear shot at him.

Bolan waited.

It didn't take long. The running footsteps of the first two men skidded outside the alley, then the steps headed for the warrior's position.

From farther down the alley the Executioner heard the second man say, "Take it easy. He can't go anywhere."

Gravel crunched under the hardman's foot when he was just a couple of steps from Bolan. The guy stopped, tensed and listened.

Bolan heard the quickening sound of the man's breathing, followed by the involuntary expulsion of breath that signaled he was steeling himself to attack.

The Executioner moved first. He took a step forward just as the man edged around the corner, leading with his weapon, an old automatic with a thick sound suppressor.

In a second Bolan took in every last detail about his attacker. His long hair framed an intense face eager for combat. Eager to kill, but not nearly accomplished enough to do it.

The warrior chopped at the man's gun hand, pinning it against the brick wall. The hardman managed to hold on to his weapon, but it was rendered useless by Bolan's grip. The sound suppressor was pointing skyward.

As soon as Bolan's left hand struck the gunman, his right hand unleathered the Beretta 93-R, aimed the weapon at his enemy's chest and fired.

The first bullet caught the hardman in the breastbone and knocked him back against the wall. His grip broke, and the automatic fell from his fingers.

Tracking upward, Bolan squeezed off a kill shot that added a 9 mm eye to the hardman's forehead.

The gunner's death left a suddenly cautious companion alone in the alley.

"Gifford," the other man whispered as he moved farther into the alley. "What happened? You okay?"

Bolan gripped the back of the dead man's shirt and bunched it into a knot. Then he slowly lifted the man from where he'd fallen.

"Gifford?" The voice was lower this time. "Gifford? Are you there?"

When there was no response, the man started to work his way back toward the mouth of the alley. He clicked on the radio and called in the backup team. "Gifford's down. Move in. Hurry."

Bolan waited until the man clicked off the radio, then he barked out his terms to the lone gunman. "Gifford's gone. Drop your weapon now and you can live."

Dead silence.

"Or you can join him," Bolan warned.

The hardman didn't want to fight it out alone with the man he thought he'd trapped.

But he didn't want to give up, either, not with reinforcements coming. Bolan had wanted to take the man alive, if possible, to see just how much Carib Command knew.

But now he just had to take him any way he could. If the man lived, fine. If not, that was the way it had to be. Bolan flicked the fire selector on the Beretta to 3-round bursts.

With a sudden shove Bolan propelled the corpse across the alley.

The man died all over again, struck by bullets from his partner's silenced weapon. His body jerked sideways from the impact before it crashed into the wall.

While the long-haired man was falling, Bolan edged around the corner and triggered a 3-round burst, tracking from right to left.

The silenced rounds thwacked into the hardman's head, tilting his neck back and driving him to the ground as though he'd been clotheslined.

Both arms flapped out to his sides. He dropped the silenced automatic, and the small radio went flying against the wall. It hissed and crackled in a last burst of static before clattering to the ground.

The two men of the Carib Command backup team thundered into the alley, expecting to help their partners pick up the pieces.

They came to a sudden halt when they saw the bloody remains of the radioman at their feet. Looking farther down the alley, they spotted Bolan standing in the shadows with his Beretta 93-R staring them in the eye.

"Move and you're dead," the warrior growled.

The two men looked at each other, silently communicating their next move.

It was their last.

As they started to raise their weapons, a dilapidated gray utility van screeched to a stop behind them, kicking up a cloud of dust as it sealed off the alley.

One of the men turned just as the vehicle's sliding door opened. Shepard fired from inside, taking out the closer man with a burst from his silenced Heckler & Koch submachine gun.

Bolan dropped the remaining gunner with a burst that stitched him from his overabundant gut to his breastbone.

The hits were practically simultaneous, with both the Executioner and Shepard instantly analyzing the kill zone and taking out their respective targets.

"That was cutting it close," the warrior commented as Shepard and two other men from his cleanup crew jumped into the alley.

"Yeah, well," Shepard said, "plans change. I was hoping we could have a talk with one of the shooters."

"They weren't in the mood. Guess they thought I was easy game."

Shepard nodded. "We picked up the other two on the monitors. Figured you could take care of the first two like we arranged. And we didn't want to scare away the others until they committed themselves to the chase."

Bolan helped Shepard and his crew load the bodies and their scattered weaponry into the back of the van. When they were all on board, Shepard closed a curtain on the dead quartet.

"So much for the welcoming committee," the operative said. "Hell of a way to start a holiday."

The Executioner nodded his head back at the curtain. "Think how they feel."

"Point taken."

"What've you got in mind for them?"

"Now we make them disappear as far from this street as possible—like this never happened. If we're lucky, they didn't have time to make a report to Carib Command about stumbling onto you near our premises. Then we get to keep running our operation here for a while longer, and you get to go back to your hotel and play world traveler for a few days before they come after your head. If we're not lucky—"

"Then we'll have to make our own luck," Bolan said.

"From what I've seen—and from what our Washington friend tells me—you're pretty good at that."

"I do what I can."

"Let's hope your luck holds up. Or else we'll all be living out of safehouses until this war is over."

Shepard left one man behind to sanitize the alley and wipe out any trace of Carib Command's presence.

Then he drove the van slowly away, listening to Caribbean music on the radio as though he didn't have a care in the world—or four dead gunmen in the back of the van.

Bolan used the time to strip off his bloodied shirt and change into the work shirt he'd appropriated from the shop.

When they were a good distance from the location of the hit, Shepard pulled the van onto the sandy shoulder of road near a seaside restaurant.

He pointed to a light blue convertible Jeep in the parking lot. "There's your new ride," he said, dropping a set of car keys into Bolan's hand.

"What about the rental I had?"

"One of my people will take it back when things cool down. No sense in taking any unnecessary risks. Some of the Carib Command gunmen might have connected you to the car."

"Understood," Bolan replied. "But what about the Jeep? Who's listed as the owner?"

"It's a company car," Shepard said. When he saw the wary look on Bolan's face, he said, "Not an *Agency* car. It's chartered to one of our subsidiary companies, a travel bureau that handles all-inclusive packages for its clients from airfare to carfare."

"Not connected to your import chain."

Shepard shook his head. "Not a chance. It's clean. It's gassed up and tuned up. That thing will move if you need it."

"Sounds like a fair trade." Bolan handed over the keys to the rental.

"That's it, then," Shepard told him. "From here on in you can fly solo. But if you need help or information, we're only a phone call away."

"Thanks." Bolan shook hands with the covert specialist, then picked up the brown leather briefcase with the spare clips that Shepard had brought along.

He climbed out of the van and headed for the parking lot. By the time he dropped the briefcase onto the Jeep's passenger seat and sat behind the wheel, the van was gone.

3

Night fell upon the island, bringing with it a cloud of insects and a cool breeze that swept in from the sea.

Bolan sat crouched in a cluster of palm trees than flanked the cliffside overlook two miles outside of Cape Brethren. It was the same spot he'd stopped at two days earlier when he'd first arrived.

It was the perfect sight for a rendezvous with Colonel Jacques Mantrell, the ISF chieftain—close enough for Bolan to get there on foot, remote enough to make contact without being seen.

Though the moon was shining brightly on the forested ridge, the Executioner was hidden safely in the shadows, clad in night gear and a black seaman's cap.

Bolan scanned the area with the compact night-vision scope that he'd brought through customs as an attachment on one of his cameras.

Traffic was sparse, with only a few cars making the trek from the bright lights below, rushing by the overlook every five or ten minutes.

And then he spotted the car he was waiting for. A gray Mercedes. It pulled off the road and eased across the gravel bed of the overlook, headlights sweeping across the curved railing at the edge. The driver turned off the lights and plunged the area back into darkness.

Bolan waited until the driver flicked the dim parking lights on and off twice before reaching inside his black Windbreaker and unclipping the miniflashlight from his shirt pocket. He pushed the button briefly, shining the light through the red lens he'd attached earlier.

Then he started walking through the woods.

The rear door of the Mercedes opened. Mantrell stepped out onto the gravel and headed toward the railing. He wore a light summer suit, well tailored to his sturdy frame.

But even in genteel plain clothes, there was nothing that could mask his military bearing. His hair was cropped short, a crew-cut shadow above a regal face with rigid features. His mixed ancestry was a tapestry of the island's history: Mayan, islander, African.

Bolan stepped quietly from cover, keeping the man between himself and the Mercedes as he walked forward.

"Mr. Belasko?" the colonel said. "Striker?"

"Colonel," Bolan replied.

Glancing at the Executioner's hands in the pockets of his Windbreaker, Mantrell said, "You can take your hand off your weapon. I'm not an impostor."

Bolan nodded. "I can't imagine anyone wanting to take your place these days." He glanced at the Mercedes, where the chauffeur was silhouetted in the window. "Tell your man to stand down, and we can call it a deal."

The colonel laughed and gave the all-clear sign to his driver. "You're a cautious man, Striker."

Bolan shrugged. "Business as usual. If I were in your position, I'd have a man cover me, too."

"I'm glad we think alike," Mantrell said, reaching out his hand. "We're going to have to work closely on this."

The warrior returned the strong handshake, then followed the colonel to the Mercedes. As soon as they climbed into the back seat, the driver flicked on the headlights and rolled back to the road. Once under way, Mantrell got down to business.

"Interesting things have been happening on the island since you got here." He looked at Bolan with a practiced, almost accusing gaze.

"We live in interesting times."

"Apparently four members of Carib Command have vanished into thin air. Our informants tell us that the leadership of the cartel is greatly concerned."

"Maybe they ran into some kind of Bermuda Triangle situation," Bolan suggested.

Mantrell smiled. "I think it's much more down-to-earth than that. Their disappearance coincided with your appearance, which happened to be two days before you were scheduled to arrive."

"Just doing a bit of homework," Bolan said.

"I expected you to check in with me the moment you got here."

"Normally I would." He explained how the gunners had been waiting for him near Shepard's import operation and how the scene was sanitized.

"There were some reports of a disturbance in the area but nothing concrete," Mantrell said.

"Maybe we got away with it this time. But somewhere along the line, the operation's been compromised. Too many people know about Shepard, and too many people know you've brought in an outsider. That's why I took my time before contacting you. I spent the past couple of days seeing if my cover held up. So far, it has.''

"Good," Mantrell said. "Then we can still execute the plans we have in mind for you. I'll tell you all about them when we get to Government House.''

The Mercedes sped downhill, then took a side road that bypassed much of the town and wound through suburbs that ran like a pastel-colored string across the cape.

Twenty minutes later they reached the complex known as Government House.

It was built on a lush strip of land that faced the sea. Like many other seats of government in the Caribbean, the colonial, pillared structure was painted pink and white, the seashell colors of a tropical paradise.

But there were other signs that paradise was falling on rough times. Floodlights illuminated most of the grounds, where several uniformed guards stood on watch.

The driveway approaching the complex was newly laid out in zigzag curves lined with concrete rails about two feet high. Though the sculptured railings were brightly painted and had flourishing plants atop some of the pedestals, it was obvious they were barricades designed to prevent vehicles from building up enough speed to smash through the gates.

The glass lanterns on the iron fence served double duty as security monitors trained on the outside perimeter. This was the landscape of a nation at risk.

The Mercedes passed through the gate check, then drove into a garage at the side of the complex. The driver parked near a well-lit bank of elevators flanked by hard-eyed island counterparts to the U.S. Secret Service.

"Here we are," Colonel Mantrell announced, pointing at the elevator. "Next stop the war room."

"Wait a minute," Bolan said, catching the colonel's shoulder before he could open the door. "This seems a bit too high profile. How many people are we dealing with in there?"

"A select few. To start with, it will be just you and me in the briefing. Maybe one or two more if necessary."

"Does that include the prime minister?"

"For now he's keeping his distance for deniability's sake. But he might have to become directly involved in some of the decision making as events progress."

"When the bullets really start to fly," Bolan said grimly.

Mantrell nodded. "I'm afraid you're right. I wish we could avoid open warfare, but at least we'll be ready for it when it happens. Now, if you don't mind..." He pushed open his side door.

Before getting out of the car, Bolan slipped on a pair of tinted nonprescription glasses and raised the collar of his Windbreaker. Then he lowered the cap so that less of his face was visible. They were just minor adjustments but would help keep him from being identified too easily.

"You can trust my people," the colonel said.

"I'm not worried about the people directly under your control, Colonel. It's the ones above you I'm thinking about. The ones out of control."

Mantrell shrugged, led him into the elevator and used his key to start it.

Bolan glanced at the panel. There were six levels for a four-story complex, which most likely meant two sublevels of bunkers and escape tunnels.

The elevator descended one floor, then the door opened onto a wide, carpeted corridor with several closed doors and an internal bank of elevators.

Standing off to the side from the open elevator well was an armed guard in khaki uniform. Hanging from a strap around his slender frame was a 9 mm Spectre submachine gun with a 50-round magazine.

A serious weapon for a sustained firefight, Bolan thought. Mantrell's people were preparing for the worst.

Despite the guard's seemingly casual stance, the man had positioned himself so that the business end of the subgun was trained toward the elevator.

When he saw Bolan standing next to Mantrell, the guard looked at the colonel until some undetectable signal passed between them. Then he lowered his weapon.

Mantrell led the way to another corridor, which ended at a wide double-door suite. The main room resembled a small museum, with several Caribbean artifacts on the tabletops and mounted on the walls— wooden statues, jade figurines and ornately painted weapons and tools.

Off of the main room was a screening room with a large conference table and a wall-length counter laden with state-of-the-art electronics gear. Sitting on top of the table was a video deck and projection television unit pointed at a large screen on the opposite wall.

While Mantrell loaded a videotape, Bolan dropped into a seat at the middle of the table with his back against the wall and his eyes on the only door into the room.

"I'm sure you know the basics," the colonel said. "I explained as much of the situation as possible to Mr. Brognola during my visit to Miami."

"Hal filled me in," Bolan said. "I've picked up a bit more Intel since I got here."

"This'll show you what we're up against." The colonel pressed the Play button to start the tape.

The videotape was evenly focused to begin with, clearly showing the troop transport helicopter hovering above the treetops. Then the commandos sailed down the ropes.

In the background the camera captured some members of the expedition looking up with surprise at the sudden descent of so many armed men.

Mantrell froze the tape and zoomed in on a woman who was hanging back from the rest, cautiously watching from the woods. "That's Karen Holmes," he said. "She's one of the survivors."

He started the tape again. By now the civilians definitely were showing unease at what was happening. Some of them looked toward the armed guard who was approaching the first group of landed commandos.

Then the first shot was fired, and the guard fell in front of the stunned civilians.

Their faces were suddenly painted with horror as the slaughter began.

That was when the video camera tracked wildly across the scene in a chaotic barrage of images: men and women screaming; commandos firing; smoke filling the air.

The tape reflected the mental state of the man who had stumbled upon the scene on his return to the site. Panic. Chaos.

It sickened Bolan to watch the tape of Carib Command gunmen methodically killing the civilians. But he forced himself to watch, imprinting every face in his memory, every movement. It might come in handy when he went after this crew of cutthroats.

Periodically Mantrell froze the tape and zoomed in on the faces of the gunmen. Some of them seemed to be acting in a form of shock themselves. Others were obviously savoring the hunt.

When the tape came to an end, several digitally enhanced images appeared on screen, close-ups of individual gunmen.

"We've identified most of them," Mantrell said. "This is Gordon Parker, the leader of this particular crew. He was attached to the Island Defense Force in one capacity or another for several years and was crooked in damn near every one of them. Turns out he was providing weapons and intelligence to the leader of the cartel."

Another man appeared on the screen. In contrast to the other images, he was in evening clothes, sitting at a table in an upscale nightclub. His hair was silver, and his eyes were ice. Though he was somewhere in his fifties, he looked physically intimidating, an arrogant man impressed with his own strength and eager for a chance to demonstrate his superiority. Surrounding him were laughing women in low-cut gowns and hard-eyed men, all of them bought and paid for.

"That's Dedrick Cambruna, leader of Carib Command. He's been implicated in fraud, embezzlement and the 'disappearance' of his enemies and witnesses who could testify against him. He went underground just before his trial was scheduled to begin, but he still wields most of the power. There are a few others vying for the top spot in their circle, but he is the real power, the one who calls the shots.''

Mantrell clicked the control button to zoom in on Cambruna's face. It seemed as if he were almost aware of the camera and was challenging anyone who dared to look at him. He had the eyes of a man who knew how to break someone, to find a weakness and exploit it in an instant.

''Cambruna's been smart so far. He usually keeps his distance from the soldiers in Carib Command, and he always stays on the move. Through his front companies he owns houses, yachts and clubs all across the islands.''

''He must have a hell of a lot of logistical support to move around like that,'' Bolan commented.

Mantrell nodded. ''He does. Both legit and underworld. He has some friends in the police and he *had* a lot of friends in the IDF until we cashiered or imprisoned most of them. We've launched several operations against him, but he always seems to have enough warning to evade us.

''Unfortunately,'' Mantrell continued, ''he is admired by many people in our country who've fallen for this Carib Command nonsense. It is a clever ruse designed to win over the disaffected and the politically unsophisticated.''

''What's the platform?''

''Carib Command says it is making the island safe for its own people, safe from outside influence and foreign intervention. They neglect to mention their real aim is to make this island a safe haven for drug dealers, murderers and would-be dictators. If Cambruna can't buy the government, he will topple it.''

"Cambruna's our ultimate target, then," Bolan said. "But if he's as unreachable as you say, we'll have to start rolling up his peripheral operations in order to get at the center. Starting with Parker's crew."

The colonel exhaled slowly as he advanced the tape to more images of Carib Command gunmen. "We are trying to locate them now. But since they struck at the ruins, the entire team has gone into hiding."

"Their kind always surface sooner or later," Bolan said. "They come out to let off steam, celebrate their victory and brag to everyone about their prowess. It's only a matter of time before you or I see them. Run the tape by me again."

Mantrell rewound the tape and once more showed the gallery of killers.

"Stop right there," Bolan said when the tape focused on the American mercenary who'd been identified as Travis Lathrop. "This Lathrop guy—according to Karen Holmes, he's responsible for helping her live through the massacre. What's your Intel on him?"

"Just what Karen told us and what we've seen on tape. He saved her, but he didn't try to stop the others from slaughtering the rest of the civilians."

"So in his mind he probably considers himself only half-guilty," Bolan said. "Someone who got in over his head. That means we can either drown him or throw him a line to save him."

"He doesn't strike me as the hero type," Mantrell said. "I don't like using his kind."

"I don't like it, either," Bolan replied, "but it's worth making an approach. If he can lead us to Cambruna, then that's the road we take."

Mantrell considered the proposition. "We'll probably need at least one of them," he agreed. "If we can turn him and he's in a position to help us, then I'm willing to make a deal with him. As for the others in the hit team—''

"They're dead. They just don't know it yet."

The colonel continued briefing Bolan on the key players in the islands, beginning with the known Carib Command gunmen and their sympathizers. Then he detailed the numbers and capacity of the vetted covert units he could send against the cartel, the ones he could trust with his life.

"As you can see," Mantrell said, "the numbers aren't very encouraging."

Bolan nodded.

"That is one of the reasons I've asked you here tonight. We can't risk waiting any longer without retaliating against Carib Command for its attack on the ruins. If Cambruna thinks we are powerless, he will grow bolder and there'll be more innocent blood shed."

"You have a target in mind?"

"Yes," Mantrell said. "Our informants have picked up on a possible meeting place of several members of the cartel's high command."

Bolan paused for a few moments, thinking over the situation. "Have you had this kind of intelligence before?"

Mantrell shook his head. "Not of this magnitude. Not with so many high-level people gathered in one spot."

"A bit coincidental. Carib Command knows you'll be looking for revenge, and all of a sudden this crucial information falls in your hands."

"Of course it's coincidental," Mantrell agreed. "But sometimes it happens that way."

"And sometimes it doesn't. Did it occur to you this might be a setup designed to neutralize some of your covert teams?"

"That's exactly what I thought at first," Mantrell said. "That's why I want you to go on the operation."

"Why's that?"

"If the information is genuine, a man of your experience can improve our chances of making a successful strike."

"And if it's a setup..."

"Then you'll improve our chances of a successful escape."

There was yet another reason for bringing Bolan into the operation. It gave Mantrell's unit a chance to see the man in action—and it gave Bolan a chance to see the caliber of ISF covert ops.

"It's a deal. Provided I can meet with the team leader beforehand and go over the ops together."

Mantrell smiled. "My man said the same thing. He's outside right now, waiting to meet *you*."

4

The seven men in night gear catfooted across the damp sand of the rock-studded beach, keeping close to the shadows of the rain forest that sprawled over the sparsely inhabited stretch of island.

They had plenty of cover for their furtive movements. A quarter moon hung dully in the sky above them. Strips of dark clouds had moved slowly overhead all night, remnants of the turbulent storm that had swept over the island earlier in the day.

A half mile ahead of them lay a cluster of fishing shacks with long wooden docks that speared out into the sea. Except for the shacks and a large sugarcane plantation farther inland, this end of the island was seldom traveled. The irregular coastline and distance from the major port areas made it too far off the beaten path for resort developers.

Which made it a plausible place for a Carib Command rendezvous, Bolan thought as he threaded his way through the slippery rocks and clutching sand.

The island was one of the lesser populated in the St. Andreas chain. It was also the southernmost, which made it a natural location for a clandestine rendezvous.

The leaders of Carib Command were meeting a new group of South American suppliers to negotiate terms for safe travel routes and transshipment of contraband—drugs, guns, illegal aliens, whatever could be moved at a good profit.

At least that was the Intel that the ISF had picked up from several of their underworld informants who moved on the periphery of Carib Command.

Bolan still felt uneasy about the operation.

The setup was almost too pat for him. For years Carib Command had managed to avoid the efforts of the island authorities to break up its operation. Now all of a sudden ISF gets hard Intel about a rendezvous.

In the pre-op briefing Bolan and his ISF counterparts had gone over every detail contained in the reports from several different informants, and all of them had corroborated the particulars of the meet—the where, the when and the why.

Could be too much of a good thing, the Executioner thought. But he couldn't afford to pass up the chance to deliver a knockout punch to Carib Command—not if he wanted to maintain good relations with his ISF counterparts.

When the small band of commandos reached a rocky ledge jutting out into the water, they were signaled to halt by their leader, Commander Granville Seward, a copper-skinned man of Indian and European descent with the build of a long-distance runner.

The others called him "Big Town," a play on words on his French name, as well as his refined worldly manner. Seward had attended university and then entered the military, a path often followed by soldier-statesmen in the Caribbean and South America.

The education didn't mean a lot to the rest of the team. Like the men in other special-forces groups Bolan had worked with, it wasn't rank that counted. It was ability. And Seward had plenty of it. He'd moved into intelligence and special operations and served as liaison with OAS, playing a key role in the joint U.S. & Organization of American States invasion of Grenada and other covert missions in the area.

While a soft hypnotic hiss of waves swept steadily over the rocks, Seward scanned the coastline with a pair of thermal-imaging binoculars, sweeping slowly back and forth over the terrain.

"Anything?" Bolan asked.

Seward looked back at Bolan with the hint of a smile on his face. "Nothing."

"Nothing that we can see."

"Take a look for yourself, Mr. Hickok," he said. "I am aware of the possibility of an ambush, but as you can see, the coast is clear."

Seward had dubbed him "Hickok" earlier when he noticed Bolan's habit of always putting himself in a position where it would be impossible for anyone to move behind him unnoticed. Playing on the cowboy image some of the island security people had of the tall and craggy-faced American warrior, Bolan had told him about the U.S. marshal who earned the name Wild Bill Hickok.

Hickok had always sat with his back against the wall so he could see any potential enemies walking into a room. The one time he'd broken his rule, Hickok was fatally shot in the back.

Bolan raised his own night-vision device, a compact Spylux night scope, and pressed the On button. He focused the eyepiece and zoomed in on the fishing shacks up ahead. The night scope's ghostlike intensified images showed him nothing but rock, sand and jungle leading up to the cluster of docks where a few small boats were tied.

"Well, Mr. Hickok?"

"Like you said," Bolan replied. "Not a soul moving. Problem is, we can't do a proper recon. The terrain up ahead is uneven. Lots of trees for cover, plenty of gullies and rocks to hide behind. Night-vision scopes can't see through rocks."

The team leader shrugged with the fatalistic acceptance Bolan had seen in many of the islanders. They'd fought against so many odds already, that if the worst happened they would be ready for it. "Aerial reconnaissance would give us away, lose any chance of surprise. Same with a patrol boat. It's a risk—but it could also be the break we've been waiting for."

Bolan nodded. Seward's eagerness was understandable. He and his men had been chasing after Carib Command for so long, they were jumping at the chance to catch them unaware.

They *had* to act on the Intel that outlined the scheduled meet, if only to keep their morale up. Bolan was also glad the operation had gotten the green light. Ever since Mantrell had introduced Seward, Bolan was impressed with how the man handled himself and how he led his men. Now he would see how well that leadership held up on the battlefield.

So far, the operation was running like clockwork. An ISF vessel outfitted with comm gear and weaponry dropped the team several miles off of the western coast. The two motorized Zodiacs that brought them the rest of the way around the southern tip of the island were now buried in the brush about a half mile back. The motors were silent running—or as silent as it was possible to make them—but there was no sense in taking a chance of beaching them too close to the target.

The Executioner glanced at his watch. Two hours remained before the meet was set to go down, which should be plenty of time to recon the area before Carib Command came in for the rendezvous.

Seward signaled the team to move forward again.

The commandos spread out on the beach, keeping plenty of space between them as they headed for the rendezvous site.

A cool breeze was at their backs, bringing with it a cloud of gnats that descended on them like a biting fog.

They ignored the sudden stings, moving fast toward their target, weapons at the ready.

The seven-man team had an array of firepower, ranging from submachine guns and grenade launchers to automatic revolving shotguns.

Bolan nosed the air in front of him with the Beretta 93-R, wire stock unfolded. His side holster carried another 9 mm pistol, and a Heckler & Koch sniper rifle was slung over his back. He was weighted for war.

THE "PRIVATE RESEARCH" vessel that was anchored in a sheltered rock-walled cove on the western side of the island was a 140-footer that at one time had belonged to the United States Navy.

When it was decommissioned and discreetly put up for auction, the only bidder was the Antilles Cargo Company, which just happened to be a corporate front for the island's fledgling navy. They were interested in quietly beefing up their own small fleet before it was outclassed by Carib Command's growing armada of high-speed powerboats and yachts.

Despite the low cost of the ship, it was in relatively good shape. In a matter of months it had been completely overhauled and outfitted with state-of-the-art surveillance gear and weaponry.

It had a dive platform and a large crane that not only enhanced its signature as a research and marine-recovery vessel, but also gave it an attack capacity. The crane could lower speedboats and motorized inflatables—like the two that had been launched earlier in the night to carry Seward's men and the American warrior that everyone had put so much faith in.

Perhaps the American *would* live up to his reputation, thought the silver-haired veteran seaman who skippered the vessel. Perhaps not. The answer would come soon enough.

As he sat in the wheelhouse idly studying the instrument panel and waiting for word from the raiding team, he exhaled a thin blue stream of pipe smoke.

War clouds, he thought. Which way would they blow? The answer would come soon enough.

The rendezvous between Carib Command and its South American partners was still an hour away. Too soon for the vessel to leave its shelter and reveal itself. They needed the element of surprise.

Once the battle started, the skipper and his hand-picked crew would sail to the target zone to aid in the assault or evacuate the raiding party.

ALL WAS CALM as the commandos drew closer to the fishing shacks. Aside from the gentle rocking of boats against the docks, there was little sound in the thick brush that crowded out the strip of beach.

Too little sound, Bolan thought when they were about one hundred yards away from their target.

Then the sky exploded.

One of Seward's men swore as a trip wire snagged his foot. A fraction of a second later a mine took it off, catching him in midair as he instinctively dived forward away from the blast.

The fiery eruption kicked him end over end in a bloody pantomime of a cartwheel. As his legs spun through the air, a gushing spout of blood poured onto the sand.

A flare cut through the darkness above them as the mine went off. The incandescent burst cascaded upon them in a deadly mushroom of light.

Adding to the shock and concussion of light and sound was a sudden barrage of autofire that ripped through the wall of trees and arced toward the beach.

The Executioner reacted instantly. As his combat sense took over, he triggered the Beretta and sent a 3-round burst toward the tree line where the first volley came from, then darted to his right.

Seward's commandos had scattered as soon as the ambush had sprung.

Several dark shapes burst from the tree line. The shapes would stop suddenly, fire at a target, then drop back out of sight while another ambusher took over.

Bolan followed his instinct and moved diagonally toward the trees, tracking the ebb and flow of gunfire as it poured back and forth on the beach with devastating effect.

On his left and right he heard bullets whapping into flesh, followed by abrupt gasps of shock.

As the fiery bursts of automatic weapons punctated the darkness, the dark shapes of the ambushers were highlighted for a moment, just long enough for Bolan to see the different pockets where the gunmen were gathered. There were at least a dozen of them. It was impossible to tell exact numbers. They sounded like a small army.

The Executioner squeezed off another burst, then dived sideways as a triburst of bullets kicked into the sand behind him.

He landed hard on the ground. The move knocked the wind out of him, but it saved him from another volley of full-auto rounds that singed the air overhead.

Bolan triggered a blast toward the briefly glimpsed shapes behind the muzzle-flashes, anticipating the moves of the ambushers and firing ahead of their lunging steps.

One of his bullets drilled into a wooden stock. Two others dropped one of the gunmen, who let out a gurgling cry for help that drew the attention of his comrades.

Bolan knelt in the wet sand and sprayed a lethal figure eight from right to left, cutting them down with a 9 mm scythe that moved like an extension of his fingertips. At that close range the Beretta was incredibly accurate.

The way the enemy muzzle-flashes were extinguished told the Executioner that his quick-reflex burst had found its mark. But the effort had emptied his clip.

Bolan shuffled sideways in a balanced crouch, planting his feet just long enough in the sand to keep up his momentum and avoid falling over while he slapped in a fresh magazine.

A stream of bullets smacked into the wet sand behind the Executioner. Spinning halfway around, he saw a white-hulled powerboat cruising just offshore, its engine growling loudly as it moved parallel to the beach.

It carried a crew full of Carib Command gunmen, who were shouting and laughing as they fired a full-auto broadside into the trapped raiders.

Only the rise and fall of the powerboat on the cresting waves kept the ISF commando team from being slaughtered. Many of the shots went nowhere near their targets.

By now Seward's men had spread out on the beach, ducking for whatever cover they could find.

"Watch out for the boats," shouted one of the commandos off to Bolan's left. "There's more coming in."

The warning was accurate, but there wasn't much the raiders could do about it. One more of Seward's men fell, cut to ribbons by several gunmen.

Bolan scanned the beach and calculated his chances of reaching cover. He was less than ten yards away from safety, a brush-covered slope that would put an embankment between him and the boatmen.

He figured he might make it, but the others were too close to the water to run the gauntlet to safety.

The Executioner doubled back and dived to the blood-soaked ground where the man who tripped the mine had fallen. He was dead now, his sightless gaze looking up into the sky.

But the weapon he'd dropped was still intact.

Bolan snatched the M-203 40 mm grenade launcher attached to the dead commando's M-16 rifle and turned to face the outlaw fleet at sea.

One of the men in the nearest powerboat either saw the Executioner as he slid the barrel forward to lock in a high-explosive round or else he had a sudden premonition of death.

Whichever it was, the man wheeled toward Bolan and blew off a full-auto burst in his direction, using tracer bullets to mark his progress toward his target.

But the target moved.

The warrior let himself drop straight back like deadweight. It was the only direction left to him that would avoid the gunfire from the man on the boat—the only one who'd noticed Bolan. The other Carib Command gunners were too busy firing on the rest of Seward's men to realize what was going on.

The Executioner was off balance as he continued falling backward. But he aimed the grenade launcher toward the back of the boat with a subconscious certainty he'd grown accustomed to on the eternal battlefield.

At just the right moment he pulled the trigger and thumped a grenade toward the dual outboard engines loudly churning the water behind the boat.

The blast echoed down the coastline, picking up volume when the gas tanks erupted and turned the powerboat into a floating incinerator.

Though the doomed men on board screamed, their desperate howls were drowned out by the all-consuming roar. Their bodies were tossed into the air like flaming and writhing bits of debris.

The sight was ghastly, but Bolan felt no pity for the men who'd gone up in flames. It was hard to sympathize with men who just a few moments before had been trying to kill you.

As the hissing wreckage sizzled into the water, the aftershock of the explosion rolled across the beach and seized the attention of the other boat teams and the ambushers on shore. That gave the surviving members of Seward's unit a chance to escape the cross fire.

"Take to the brush," Bolan shouted. "That's our only way out of here."

Seward picked up the call and alerted the other members of the team. Then he half dragged, half carried one of his wounded men toward cover.

It could have been suicidal. The only escape route left to them was guarded by men with submachine guns, but fortunately they were distracted by the explosion for a critical few moments.

Before they could concentrate on their quarry again, Bolan sprayed the bushes in front of Seward and the wounded man as they staggered across the last stretch of sand.

Then he headed for the brush himself, tucking and rolling down a sandy incline, branches slashing at his face until he grabbed onto the base of a thin tree trunk to slow his descent.

He froze, listened to the sounds all around him, then quietly moved away from the spot where he'd crashed through the brush. With a careful and silent maneuver Bolan unslung the sniper rifle from his back and secreted it near a dark mass of roots coiled around the jagged bottom of a fallen tree.

Fixing the location of the weapon firmly in mind, he continued on.

Footsteps sounded all around him, converging toward the spot where he'd entered the patch of forest. They were trying to be stealthful but weren't successful.

Bolan followed the sounds of their heavy footfalls thumping into the dirt and the soft hiss of moisture spilling from the broad green leaves still wet from the earlier storm.

To a man versed in covert operations and jungle survival, it was like listening to an organic broadcast.

He heard two of these "trackers" well before he saw them. They were dressed in regular jeans and shirts, more used to hunting for their prey in cities.

The pair of ambushers pushed through the brush less than ten yards from Bolan's position. They glanced in his direction, but the camouflage paint streaked across his face and his dark night gear made him practically invisible.

He controlled his breathing as they moved by and willed himself to become completely still.

And then he went after them, stepping softly across the clinging branches, matching his pattern with theirs. They were separated from each other by about ten feet as they moved in and out of the shadows.

As he drew closer, the Executioner heard the man in the back muttering to himself and repeating the same worried phrase over and over as if it was a mantra. "He's got to be here," he said. "He's got to be around here."

"Shut it," the other man hissed, turning and tracing the dark forest with the unmistakable thick barrel of a Sterling submachine gun, a holdover from the days when the British played a more active role in the affairs of the Caribbean island states.

"We should of found him by now."

"Keep it up, the man's going to find you."

But the ambusher wouldn't or couldn't stop speaking aloud, almost as if he were trying to convince himself of the truth of what he was saying. "It isn't making sense. We saw him come in here. Maybe he's been hit. He's hit and trying to crawl away. Maybe he's wounded," he said hopefully.

"Then maybe you stand a chance of getting out of this alive," the man with the Sterling subgun said. "You should be able to handle a half-dead man." Without saying another word, he resumed prowling for Bolan.

The warrior watched the back of his head disappear through some foliage. Then he moved in on the trailing man.

When he was about ten feet away from the gunner, Bolan stepped sideways. He crossed one foot silently over the other until he was close enough to launch himself at the target.

Bolan's left hand curved under his adversary's chin and jammed it skyward, clicking his teeth together from the impact and paralyzing him with shock. At the same time the Executioner's right hand sliced the heavy razor-edged combat knife across the gunner's throat.

It happened in a blurring motion too quick and final for the man to realize what had happened . . . until the blood from his slit throat spouted into the air.

His trachea was filleted, and he had only a handful of seconds left to live.

His eyes met the Executioner's with a look of betrayal, as if the dark-clad intruder had somehow changed the rules on him. It wasn't supposed to work out this way.

Bolan's interest in the man's eyes was tactical only, studying him long enough to make sure he was out of action forever. With a quick sweep he freed the man's submachine gun from his hands and then pushed him off to the side.

Alerted by the sound, the man with the Sterling subgun stepped back through the brush into a small clearing and peered toward Bolan's direction. His head was inclined at an awkward angle as he tried to see what his partner was up to.

By the time he realized his partner was dying, Bolan sent *him* along the same path. He lunged forward from the darkness, planted his foot onto the ground and whipped the knife across the small clearing.

The blade ripped through the muscle walls of the ambusher's chest and buried itself in his heart. His head jerked down from the motion—with his now sightless eyes appearing to stare at the black-handled knife sprouting from his flesh.

Then he dropped the subgun onto the ground and slumped forward like a freshly chopped tree.

Bolan circled around the two dead men in case any other Carib Command gunners were attracted by the commotion. With his Beretta leading the way, he filtered through the rain forest toward the next cluster of ambushers.

It didn't take long to make contact. They saw him the same time that he saw them. There were three of them when they started firing at Bolan, two of them after the warrior squeezed off a burst and moved on.

Farther down the forest he heard sudden bursts of gunfire and loud yells.

Then a temporary quiet fell again until it was suddenly broken by machine-gun chatter.

In close-quarters combat Bolan and Seward's veteran jungle fighters had the upper hand. They knew how to move quickly, strike and then vanish before the gunmen could retaliate. It took a short time before they whittled down the would-be ambushers.

After a relatively long pause Bolan shouted, "Big Town! You there?"

Seward's reply echoed from somewhere off to the left. "Over here, Hickok."

Gradually Bolan and the surviving members of the special-forces team moved toward one another, periodically calling out and checking for the enemy.

Once they regrouped they made a quick sweep through the brush. But the ambushers were either lying low, had fled for their lives or left their lives behind them, thanks to the tenacity of the veteran covert operatives.

Their more immediate threat was the small fleet of powerboats that patrolled offshore. Once the first boat had gone up in flames, the others nosed out into deeper waters. When it seemed that they were no longer threatened, they had drifted back toward land.

Four of the long powerboats were visible, laden with gun-wielding crews eager to go ashore and win back their honor.

Maybe more of the Carib Command fleet was scouting the coast on the far side of the fishing shacks.

"There's no way we can take all of them," Seward stated.

"We don't have to take them all," Bolan replied. "Just enough to hold them off for a while."

Seward had radioed the man who'd stayed behind with the inflatables to come in to pick them up at the evac zone about a half mile south of their present position.

The support vessel was also on its way. The question in all of their minds was how many of them would be left alive by the time help arrived.

If they ran for the designated rally point, the powerboats could strafe the beach and take them out. If they waited for help, the seagoing gunmen would come ashore. After waiting out the battle, they'd return to pick off a batch of bloodied and beaten men.

And they wouldn't be too far off the mark. Three of Seward's men were dead. A fourth man was wounded.

Bolan retrieved the 7.62 mm semiautomatic Heckler & Koch PSGI sniper rifle from the spot where he'd cached it earlier. Then he scurried up the small brush-covered slope and set up his position on the crest of the ridge overlooking the water.

Careful not to make any sudden movements, he spiked the bipod into the ground at the edge of the leafy cover to give himself the widest possible kill zone.

The night scope provided him with a good view of the Carib Command boatmen, and the 20-round magazine gave him a good chance to do something about it.

Seward and his second-in-command spread out on both sides of Bolan. The wounded man, whose leg was soaked with blood, lay on his back and looked up at the sky. His face was a constant mask of pain, but he fought off the agony and managed to stay silent as he clutched a Heckler & Koch submachine gun with a fresh magazine to his chest.

"We'll cover the beach," Seward said. "Just in case they make it ashore."

"There's plenty to go around," Bolan replied. "Whatever you do, just hold your fire until they get close enough for me to do the maximum damage."

The Executioner swept the barrel of the sniper rifle from left to right, sighting on the boats and studying the position of the crews on each boat until he could pick out the most important one—the man behind the wheel.

After mentally rehearsing his order of attack, Bolan spoke softly to Seward, who was propped up on the ridge just to his right. "Okay," he said, "get ready. This is it."

Bolan pressed the buttstock into his shoulder and zeroed in on the man behind the wheel of the nearest boat just as its hull rode down into a trough between the cresting waves. For one split second the wheelman's ghostlike face appeared in the cross hairs of the night-vision scope.

Then Bolan turned him into a ghost for real.

The 7.62 mm slug cored through the middle of the wheelman's forehead on a downward slant that made a large exit wound at the back of his neck. As his skull exploded, his hands lost their grip on the wheel.

While the wheel spun wildly out of control, the motion of the boat threw the dead man forward over the windscreen. Seeing their dead pilot suddenly transformed into a bloody heap started the rest of the crew scrambling for the wheel.

The first one to gain control of it was a broad-shouldered man who pushed the others out of the way and grabbed the spinning wheel with ham-sized hands.

Bolan tracked the rise and fall of the bow as it crashed through the waves, then pulled back slowly on the trigger of the sniper rifle.

The first bullet drilled into the hardman's left arm and sent a spray of blood into the air.

But the heavy man held onto the wheel.

The second shot ripped through his chest and spun him into a soulless dance down the length of the boat. Without anyone steering it, the boat swung backward toward the shore.

Bolan turned his attention to the next boat in line, a high-speed cruiser with a man on the upper deck.

It took two more shots to take the man permanently out of play.

The Executioner kept firing the semiautomatic sniper rifle with deadly accuracy, swiveling from left to right and dropping one wheelman after the next until the Carib Command force realized that anyone who attempted to steer any of the boats would receive an automatic death sentence.

"Let them know you're here," Bolan said.

Seward sprayed a full-auto burst from his submachine gun at the boats floating offshore.

The other raider opened up at the same time, adding more clamor and gun chatter to the head-spinning mix of destruction. Through it all Bolan continued firing the sniper rifle.

When the rapidly shrinking fleet realized how many hits they were taking, the boats roared toward the open sea, lurking just offshore and rolling with the waves.

"Move out," Bolan said, "before they figure out where to make a landing and come after us."

"What about you?"

"I'll stay here a while longer to try to convince them it's a bad idea to come ashore."

"But we can't just leave you."

"I don't plan on ending it here. You go ahead. I'll catch up to you when I can."

Seward hesitated, then gave Bolan a look that said that he felt responsible for leading them into the ambush and that it shouldn't be up to the grim-faced warrior to stay behind.

Bolan shrugged it off. It wasn't the first time he was dealt this kind of hand. "I've been through this before," the Executioner said. "I've got the best chance of getting us out."

"We'll wait for you at the Zodiac. Unless you want us to come for you."

"No. I'll make it down to the boat. You're traveling with a wounded man—that gives me plenty of time to catch up. If not, just leave one of the boats."

"We're not leaving without you."

"The hell you aren't," Bolan growled. "If I'm not there when you ship out, just leave one of the boats behind."

"But—"

"Just do it. Don't worry about me. I didn't come all the way down here just to die on you."

The leader of the ISF team nodded. Then he and the other man shouldered their wounded comrade and hurried off through the brush.

Bolan stayed behind, hoping to buy some time for the remnants of the raiding team and make Carib Command pay the ultimate price.

5

Bright yellow spotlights lighted up the beach.

The cones of light from the cartel fleet illuminated the bodies lying in the sand, then streamed through the brush as the powerboats cruised along the shore.

They were getting bolder now.

The Executioner had lain low after the last exchange with the Carib Command gunners. They'd come in slow with their running lights off and their engines at low throttle.

When the boats were parallel with the beach, they'd hit it with a broadsides barrage, opening up with everything they had, turning the site into a fireworks display. The Executioner stopped firing suddenly, letting them think he'd been hit and there were no more defenders left.

Now it would cost them to find out for sure.

Bolan watched as one of the powerboats broke from the others and headed toward shore, stopping several yards off the jagged coastline.

A quartet of gunmen climbed onto the bow. Holding their weapons overhead, they splashed down into the shallow water and stormed the beach.

The rest of the powerboats hung back, unwilling to commit themselves until they saw what the scouting party found.

Bolan waited, letting them think there was nothing to fear.

It didn't take long. Their caution evaporated when they encountered no opposition.

The battlefield was theirs.

With flashlights strapped to the barrels of their automatic rifles, they scanned the bodies on the shore. Yellow trails of light lingered over the bloodied forms of the ISF commandos to make sure they were dead.

A single gunshot echoed down the beach as one of the gunmen fired into the body of the commando who'd tripped over the mine.

Other gunshots followed as they carefully went from man to man, delivering insurance rounds.

The sound of the bullets striking unmoving flesh reached Bolan in sickening clarity. He felt like taking them out now, but he had to wait until they were a bit closer to the forest—too close for the men in the powerboats to provide covering fire.

It was only a matter of time.

A matter of balance.

The quartet moved toward the woods.

It was quiet. Dead quiet. The members of the land-based ambush team had either run or been wiped out.

Bolan tracked the quartet with the sniper rifle. His Beretta 93-R had a full clip, as did the automatic holstered at his side.

It was enough firepower to last them out before he exfiltrated from the kill zone.

By now Seward and the others had made it to the rendezvous with the Zodiac. Bolan could join them as long as he could keep the rest of the cartel hardmen occupied.

The flashlight beams whipped overhead, crisscrossing in dizzying patterns as the four-man squad spread out to recon the area.

The Executioner took in a long and slow breath, then just as slowly exhaled as he sighted on the man who'd been first to fire into the slain ISF commandos. He, too, would be the first.

Bolan followed the man as he walked with the sudden step of a conqueror, a man who'd drawn blood—even if it was only from someone already dead.

In a fortunate misstep the Carib Command gunman had stumbled in the sand just before Bolan squeezed the trigger. Instead of hitting him in the chest, the 7.62 mm caught him in the shoulder and spun him around.

Bolan finished him off with a second round that took off part of his head. The man completed the spin, then dropped into the sand as blood oozed from the wound to stain the ground.

At the sound of the first shot, the other men in the recon team turned toward their fallen comrade. But he was no longer in sight as the flashlight beams cut a horizontal swath of light three feet above his body.

One of the men called out to him, then swore and swung his rifle light toward the woods.

Bolan had moved several feet away and had a clear field of fire. He took the gunner down with two quick shots that toppled him over.

A burst of submachine-gun fire chopped into the woods, sailing high over the Executioner's head. A second volley followed a nanosecond later. Though both men had reacted fairly quickly, they were wide of the mark.

The man off to Bolan's left had turned off his light as soon as the firing began. Obviously the more experienced of the two fighters, he'd flicked off the flashlight switch with a swipe of his hand. He immediately moved forward from his last position and crouched low to the ground, listening to the sounds of gunfire and trying to fix in his mind where the shots were coming from.

"Don't just stand there!" he shouted at his dazed partner, who was a bit slower in turning off his light and ducking for cover. "Shoot him."

"Where *is* he, Edmund?" he shouted. "I can't see anything."

"Then shoot and find out!" Edmund hissed back at him. "Remember your training—recon by fire."

"I'll do it! I'll do it!" the other man said, firing off several short bursts that peppered the woods near Bolan. It wasn't skill or calmness that sent the bullets close to the Executioner's position.

It was panic. Panic and luck. The man was desperately shooting at shadows—shadows that Bolan had just sought for cover.

The Executioner set down the sniper rifle and moved off to his right, clutching the Beretta 93-R. He dropped into a prone position on the edge of the ridge and carefully scanned the terrain for the closest gunman, then looked out to sea where the powerboat fleet rocked up and down in the waves.

It wouldn't be long before they sent another party ashore.

Bolan had to be long gone by then.

He inched forward in the dirt, staying low and moving slowly until he had a shot at the shadowy figure who'd been killing every tree in sight.

The Executioner squeezed off a 3-round burst that sliced into the dirt at the gunman's feet. The man jumped and started to run for it.

Bolan corrected his aim and triggered another volley of slugs that climbed up and punched into the man's chest.

The warrior's deadly aim took out the other man just as his last wild burst of autofire chopped into the air. With an angry cry the dying man rose like a phantom from the sand and turned toward Edmund, shouting something through his blood-filled throat. It was one last curse at the man who had led him to his death.

Then he dropped dead into the sand.

Only one gunman remained on shore that Bolan had to deal with. But he was nowhere in sight. He'd been playing it smart, using the other gunmen as fodder, a decoy to draw Bolan's fire.

With an almost sixth sense screaming at him to move, the Executioner anchored his foot into the sand, then pushed up with all his might, diving back toward the bushes.

A streak of autofire seared the air behind him.

As he fell, Bolan triggered a return burst from the Beretta in the general direction of his attacker. It was a reflex move designed to keep his adversary from advancing close enough to finish Bolan off.

The Executioner landed facefirst in the brush. He used his forearms to break the fall, then launched himself forward through the clutching branches and thorns.

Another burst sliced through the brush behind him. The man was good. If the Executioner hadn't followed his instincts, the cartel gunman might have taken him out.

Bolan tumbled downhill through the brush, then rolled out onto a soft patch of earth. He came up in a crouch and trained his Beretta skyward.

A skeletal barrier of underbrush and ivy stood between Bolan and the surviving gunner. If the man was moving anywhere near the edge, he'd be silhouetted near the sky.

But no one was there.

The warrior's attacker was playing it careful. And that was going against Bolan. He couldn't afford to be part of a cat-and-mouse game with the man stalking him. The more time passed, the less chance Bolan had of getting off the island alive.

The Executioner had to go after him.

He dropped into the shadow of the forest and set a course parallel to the coastline, moving toward the spot where he figured the gunman had filtered into the brush.

Branches brushed at the warrior's broad shoulders as he knifed through the closely intertwined trees. Palm leaves fanned overhead as he moved his body in sync with the terrain, crouching low, turning sideways, pushing slowly forward through the dense green foliage.

The dull black barrel of the Beretta 93-R led the way like an antenna as he moved forward with only one thought on his mind—hit and git.

After a full minute of covering ground, Bolan stopped and listened for sounds of his stalker's approach.

It came a few seconds later when the man's bulky frame cut through whispering branches. The sound stopped for a few seconds before he moved on again.

The stalker was heading in Bolan's direction, but he was keeping low and staying behind cover.

The Executioner could make out his shadow, but it wasn't enough of a target to guarantee a kill.

Half-dead was good enough, Bolan thought. He stepped out of cover to get a better angle and fired a 3-round burst at the moving half-hidden target.

Two of the bullets whacked into a tree trunk and chipped off large chunks of bark.

The third bullet hit closer to home.

The stalker grunted in surprise, then dived behind cover. Bolan wasn't sure if the bullet hit him or if the splinters from tree bark had speared into the man.

A stream of flame suddenly scorched the air, and a full-auto burst of submachine-gun fire rained in his direction. Bolan moved away from the path of the bullets before the gunner could zero in on him.

Then he heard the other man grunting as he collapsed against the tree and gasped for breath.

He was wounded. And desperate.

"Come on," the other man shouted with a bull-like roar. "Let's see what you got."

He came out firing, chopping toward Bolan with a full-auto burst, cooking off the clip in his last mad dash.

Rather than panic at the giant's sudden attack, the Executioner moved to his right, curling his right arm under him as he dived parallel to the ground. He triggered a burst that struck the Carib Command gunner in the head and felled him like a tree.

As the man dropped in a bloody heap, Bolan hurried to the edge of the brush and fired a stream of bullets at the boats just to let them know the enemy still owned the beach.

Then he left the battlefield, hoping by the time they got up enough courage to send in another crew he would be out of range.

The warrior moved southward on a steady jog through the forest, picking up his speed the farther he got from the ambush site. He didn't come out onto the shoreline until he was almost at the rendezvous point.

Looking back, he saw spotlights shining from the boats onto the beach as more Carib Command hardmen stormed ashore.

Up ahead one of the sleek Zodiacs was nosing out into the water, piloted by the ISF commando Granville Seward had tasked with picking up the raiding team.

Bolan called out to them, shouting his name so they wouldn't turn and fire on the dark figure racing toward them, splashing loudly through the surf that crashed at his feet.

Seward stood up in the inflatable and anchored himself on one of the lifelines. "Come on," he shouted, reaching out for the Executioner.

The warrior took several more steps, plunging waist deep in the water before catching Seward's hand and diving into the Zodiac.

The small craft headed out into the open sea.

THE VESSEL APPEARED like a ghost ship on the horizon, its silhouetted shape rising and falling with the waves.

The "research" vessel cut through the water at high speed, transforming itself into a warship every step of the way as it bore down on the inflatable, responding to the light signals sent by Seward.

Retractable .50-caliber machine guns emerged from their wells and were locked into place.

A rifle team deployed along the deck's railing.

An ISF gunner took up his position behind a 20 mm automatic cannon and zeroed in on the powerboats lurking in the distance. After their fruitless search on-shore, the Carib Command ambush team took to their go-fasts once again and sent part of the fleet after the Zodiac that had exfiltrated the ISF team.

From his post in the wheelhouse, the silver-haired skipper of the ship spoke softly into the microphone, relaying his command to the men at the battle stations. "Let them know we're here."

The automatic cannon spit fire as the 20 mm shells arched over the sea and thumped into the water near the lead boat of the cartel armada. He adjusted the trajectory and dropped 20 mm rivets onto the hull.

The sustained fire of the automatic cannon stitched the powerboat from bow to stern. Both of its outboard motors exploded in a nova of flame that launched the Carib Command passengers up in the air like disintegrating human rockets.

As the 140-footer closed the gap, the machine gunners opened up with the .50-calibers, punching tracer rounds across the dark sky toward the oncoming powerboats.

When the cannon kicked in again, strafing the front of the convoy, the Carib Command fleet suddenly broke.

The high-speed powerboats turned back the other way, leaving off the pursuit of the small team in the Zodiac.

A few minutes later the Zodiac pulled alongside the ISF ship. While Bolan and the others secured the inflatable to the cargo nets hanging over the side, the crew of the rescue ship maneuvered a crane in place and lowered a caged-in stretcher for the wounded man.

As soon as the man was hoisted aboard into the hands of the ship's medics, the rest of the raiding party clambered up the cargo nets.

The skipper was on deck to help them aboard—and to see which of them hadn't made it back. During the relatively short time of the mission, his face appeared to have aged several years.

He'd known the men well, and he also knew how much the strapped ISF needed each one of them.

Granville Seward wasn't the same man, either. He'd led this same ISF unit on several previous ops with only the rare casualty. Now half of his team was out of action.

Tactically it was a blow to the covert forces. Seward's team was ranked at the top of the ISF units.

It was also a blow to his spirit. The inevitable guilt and second-guessing was overwhelming. If he'd been more cautious... if he'd been more skeptical of the intelligence they had... if he came in with more men...

Seward fought off his sorrow for the time being as he and Bolan followed the skipper back into the wheelhouse for a debriefing.

As soon as they were inside, the craggy-faced seaman shook his head. "They were waiting for us all along. And we walked right into it."

"No," Seward said, "I led them into it." He looked at Bolan for his response, half expecting an I-told-you-so.

"We had to check it out," the warrior replied. "It could have been the jackpot."

"It could have been the graveyard for all of us," Seward retorted. "Not just the ones we left behind."

"It happened," Bolan said. "Let's deal with it and get on with what we have to do next."

The rest of the briefing was short. There was little percentage in chasing after the cartel's powerboat fleet. The gunmen they'd faced tonight obviously weren't the higher-echelon leaders they were hoping to find. This had been a military arm of Carib Command, nothing more than hired guns and trained killers.

Perhaps the best the cartel could field against them.

"*They* left a lot behind, too," Bolan said. "We hit them pretty hard."

Seward nodded. "Yeah, we did at that. Hard enough to send a message to Dedrick Cambruna that he's got a war on his hands."

The vessel steered a course back to the island, heading straight for the ambush site to recover the bodies of the slain ISF operatives.

Seward had led his men there, and now he would bring them back.

6

A row of tall palm trees swayed in the wind, their slender trunks bending like graceful swan necks.

Below the trees sat clusters of white wooden beach chairs, positioned around glass-topped tables covered with flickering candles, green bottles of imported beer, Caribbean-brewed Red Stripe and stout bottles of rum.

No brightly colored tourist drinks. This was one of the down-home night spots favored by the islanders, a few daring visitors and the St. Andreas underworld.

Situated at the end of a long strip of Cape Brethren clubs, it was rustic and raucous.

Ska music boomed from the open doors of the enclosed nightclub area and drifted across the open-air terrace that slanted down to a seawall at the water's edge.

Sun-bronzed waitresses in clinging white cotton dresses moved through the crowd, quickly replenishing drinks and snatching away half empties.

Half the outside crowd was roaring drunk, and the other half was in the process of getting there. Couples were dancing to the music that flowed out to the beachfront. So were singles. Some of the women who had had too much to drink fell into the arms of men who had a hard time standing themselves.

Anyone and everyone was moving to the infectious beat of the horn-tinged ska music. Especially the three men from Gordon Parker's hit team that Bolan had been following for most of the night.

They'd been womanizing and wandering all over Cape Brethren, hitting the bars and bordellos alike in a hurry to spend the blood money they'd earned from the massacre at the ruins.

A few other members from the helicopter assault team had also appeared around town. Shepard's people had spotted them, and so had members of the ISF.

But the ISF surveillance was low-key. Since many of Colonel Mantrell's men were known to former IDF members who'd defected to Carib Command, the government watchers stayed in the background, observing what they could. They were street men only, tasked with passing the information on to the action arm.

The Executioner.

Even terrorists had days off, Bolan thought as he watched the trio of men fuel their high-octane drunk by passing around a bottle of rum until it was dead.

He scanned the area again, searching for Gordon Parker's face. But the leader of the hit team was nowhere in sight. He was most likely playing it safe, keeping half of his handpicked killers under lock and key until the other half returned from leave.

An iffy proposition.

When the band ended its set and a temporary silence settled on the beach, Bolan followed the three men as they pushed their way through the outside crowd and headed back into the main clubhouse.

A cannabis haze swirled overhead, chopped into wispy fragments by a four-bladed propeller fan.

Once inside, the trio of gunmen hurried to a just-vacated table near the bar and stared down two men who'd been heading for it at the same time.

The two men walked away, figuring it was better to stand somewhere else than get their teeth knocked out by three out-of-control toughs.

Bolan waited until the crowd at the bar shifted, then took a spot at the end of the counter where he could hear the Carib Command hit men.

He sat with his back to them, peripherally watching their reflections in the mirror.

Since he'd poured his last one into the sand outside, Bolan ordered another glass of rum from an extremely busy barmaid who barely had time to register what her customers looked like, let alone what they ordered.

Bolan sat hunched over the drink, biding his time. From what he'd seen, it wouldn't be long before the men ran out of money. They'd been throwing it around all night as if they were landed gentry instead of guns-for-hire.

It happened about twenty minutes after the trio of Carib Command islanders had taken their place at the table. A small argument broke out among them about who was going to pay for the next round. None of them had a dollar left.

"Go out to the car," the loudest and brawniest of the three men said. "Get some smoke. Get some powder. We'll sell it or trade it."

The man he was speaking to shook his head. "I'm off duty today," he said. "I don't take orders from anybody."

"From me, you do."

"Not tonight, I don't," the other man replied, shaking his head. He was much taller than either of his partners, and much drunker, which gave him the courage to refuse.

"All right, all right," the third man said. "I'll do it, just to keep you girls from crying all night long." He pushed his chair back and got unsteadily to his feet. His eyes scanned the room as if he'd just discovered a new land or had wandered into some kind of new dimension. But then he shook it off and got his bearings.

The intoxicated hit man grabbed his jacket from the back of the chair and shook it until he heard the jangling of his car keys. Then he lurched toward the front door. "Be right back," he said.

Bolan waited about twenty seconds until a pair of bar girls sauntered past and caught the attention of the remaining two gunmen. Then he drifted into the crowd and headed out the door.

A string of parked cars stretched all the way from the front door of the nightclub up to a distant clay-and-grass lot shrouded by trees. Most of the cars were older models with the traditional house-paint colors, but some of them were late models with lots of chrome gleaming in the moonlight.

Totally unnoticed by the Carib Command hit man, Bolan caught up with him near the shade of one of the trees.

The Executioner stayed back in the shadows, his black clothes blending with the night. He watched the man crouch over and fumble with his keys as he tried to unlock the door of a black Mercury.

It took several tries before the man found the right one and grunted with victory as he fitted the key into the slot.

"All right," the man said as the door lock flipped up. He reached for the handle—and suddenly saw the reflection of his face hurtling toward his eyes.

It didn't make sense to him. It was happening too fast for him to react, let alone realize that his past had caught up to him in sudden and final form.

Bolan's right hand cupped the back of the man's head and rapped it into the hard glass. The Carib Command gunner flopped on the ground near the car.

The Executioner picked up the man's jacket, then pushed him under the car until he was out of sight and his body was merged with the shadows.

TEN MINUTES LATER two angry men headed for the Mercury. They saw a huddled form apparently asleep behind the wheel, with his jacket propped behind his head like a pillow.

"Look at him!" the bullnecked hit man growled. "Bastard's fallen asleep." He tugged on the door handle, but the driver's side was locked. "Come on!" he shouted, pounding his knuckles on the window. "Wake up. Open this freakin' door."

"It's no use, Alden," the taller man said. "You know what he's like when he passes out. Nothing's going to wake him. Let's go back inside. I'm thirsty."

"And use *what* for money?" Alden asked. "That's why we came out here in the first place, Joseph."

"Okay, right. Don't worry."

Joseph made a circuit of the car until he reached the front passenger door and found it unlocked. Swinging it wide open, he stuck his head inside and shouted, "Hey, wake up, man!" His shout turned to shock as he realized the man behind the wheel wasn't his friend.

Bolan slid the silenced Beretta from under his black Windbreaker and pointed it at the man's forehead. "Get into the car," he ordered.

"No!" the man shouted, digging for his hardware. "You're craz—"

A 9 mm round from the Beretta burrowed through the bridge of the man's nose and kicked him backward. His long arms flailed wildly in a jerky puppetlike gesture as his fingers opened and closed while trying to grasp onto one last shred of life.

Then he dropped flat on his back onto the ground.

Alden was caught between his urge to run and his urge to avoid a similar fate. Bolan made the decision for him. "One second to get in," he said, "or one second to die."

"All right ... Don't freak out. Don't shoot. I'm getting in. We can work something out here."

"Maybe," Bolan said as the man climbed into the passenger seat. "Close the door."

Alden obeyed.

"Clock's running. You have one minute to convince me not to shoot you."

"Okay. Stay cool. I'm understanding you here." Despite his words, Alden clearly didn't understand he was out of his league. His eyes moved left and right as he sized up the man in black and looked for an opening.

It was obvious that in the past his sheer bulk had allowed him to muscle his way out of enough tight situations that he thought he could do the same here.

"Talk," Bolan ordered.

"Right, right. You're in charge. Whatever you want, you can have. We've got a full brick we can lay on you—" He tapped the glove compartment. "It's right in here."

Bolan smiled. "Yeah. I saw the coke. I also saw the pistol in there. Take your hand away from the glove compartment."

"But—"

"Take it away or *lose* it."

Alden complied quickly. "So maybe you don't want the coke," he said. "What do you want."

"I want Dedrick Cambruna." The Executioner waved the silenced barrel of the Beretta back and forth so it tracked across the wide forehead of his prisoner.

"Cambruna!" Alden's eyes widened, as if the mention of the name had conditioned him to react in abject fear.

"Yeah, Cambruna," Bolan repeated. "Can you give him to me?"

"No. It's impossible. I've only seen him a couple of times."

"What about Parker?"

"Parker," he said, trying to sound as though he was greatly relieved. "Now, that is a different matter. Parker is someone I can give to you."

It was obviously a lie. Bolan could see it in the man's eyes. He couldn't deliver Cambruna. He couldn't even deliver Parker. Instead, he was trying to throw Bolan off the track while he got ready to attack.

The man turned to his right, shaking his head as if he were ashamed at himself for caving in so easily to Bolan's demands. His left hand suddenly snapped out at Bolan's head. The huge ham fist would have cracked his skull if it connected, or at least given him enough time to fish the pistol out of the glove compartment.

But Bolan ducked forward just as the bigger man moved. At the same time he moved his gun hand to the right.

Their arms passed each other like swords crossing in a duel. But Bolan's arm had a fully loaded Beretta at the end of it.

The soft cough of the silencer sounded twice.

The gunman became a dead man. His head dropped forward, revealing a growing pattern of blood splattered on the seat and the window.

Bolan loaded the other two gunmen into the back seat of the Mercury, then drove slowly from the parking lot. He took the road that led south out of town, up into the winding roads he'd first scouted on his arrival in Cape Brethren.

He drove until he reached a section of road that jutted out from the mountain in a sharp turn that overlooked a steep cliff. There was nothing but rock and sea below.

The Executioner slowed, killed the lights, then pulled off onto the rough gravel shoulder. He eased the car forward and took it almost to the edge of the drop-off before he stopped and put the car into Park.

Spinning the steering wheel all the way to the right, Bolan opened the driver's door and stepped halfway out of the car. Keeping one foot on the brake, he leaned back inside and shifted the lever into Drive.

Then he bailed out.

With a sudden lurch the front wheels of the Mercury jumped over the edge. When the front end of the car tilted forward, the chassis hit the edge with a loud crunching sound.

Metal groaned against stone, then the black vehicle toppled end over end before crashing into the rock-studded surf below.

As the sound of the crash echoed briefly against the cliff, the car sank out of sight.

The warrior stayed near the edge of the cliff for a few minutes, watching to see if the car resurfaced.

Then he began the long trek back down into Cape Brethren, a black-clad shadow jogging alongside the empty road.

Though the disappearance of the three men would soon be noticed, there were two things going in Bolan's favor.

If the car was found before the bodies were consumed by undersea scavengers, there would be plenty of bar crawlers who'd seen the men in their inebriated state.

It was impossible not to have noticed the three toughs staggering up and down the Cape Brethren strip. They'd had a couple of drunken scuffles that ended up with a few less-hardy souls lying unconscious in the street.

In their condition, an accident like this—especially on the treacherous hills outside of Cape Brethren—was a totally plausible scenario. If the bodies were recovered intact, the bullet holes might cause some trouble.

Bolan figured he had a day or two before the Carib Command leadership realized that they either had a few more casualties or some of their men had gone AWOL. That was the second thing in the warrior's favor. No matter how well trained Gordon Parker's crew was, some of them were still hired guns who considered a few days of berserker R&R as a vital part of their training.

THE BRIGHT PURPLE bikini top hung like a captured flag from the fly bridge of the sport-fishing boat anchored five hundred yards offshore in the light blue waters of Dunwick Bay.

Lying topless on the foredeck was the owner of the iridescent top, a deeply tanned woman with long black hair. Her slender arms were folded behind her neck as she leaned against the windscreen, a voluptuous sea nymph recruited from one of the hotels that ringed the bay.

Next to her, the chiseled muscles of his stomach and chest seared to a lobster-red tint by the afternoon sun, lay Sidney Lisle, a member of Gordon Parker's airborne assault team—paratrooper, ex-legionnaire, ex-convict, soldier of fortune.

He was a Frenchman addicted to wine, women and war. His tours of duty in East Africa and the Indian Ocean had usually been brought to an abrupt end in a cloud of scandal, intrigue and atrocity. It was always the same—when legitimate government authorities and war-trial tribunals came into the area, Sidney Lisle moved on to the next theater of war.

He was a known commodity to the merchants of death who farmed out their specialists all across the world, a man who could be reached by a phone call and a promise of booty. It was the spoils of war that had brought him down to the Caribbean, and the chance of starting a new life.

His past was largely unknown to the authorities in the area. And if things worked out right, the next authorities on the island would be the very same people he was working for.

His current employers recognized a kindred spirit in the hard-edged Frenchman.

Lisle had a simple philosophy about life and death. If soldiers fell because of his actions, then it was simply a matter of their luck running out. If civilians fell—like the members of the archaeological expedition excavating the St. Andreas ruins—then it was dumb luck, their own fault.

They should have known better than to get in the way of Sidney Lisle and his paycheck. A man had to make his living, no matter how much killing was involved.

As the boat bobbed up and down in the water in a gently lulling motion, Lisle turned up the volume of a waterproof cassette player fastened to the deck with a suction cup.

The jet skis and high-powered watercraft whining through the bay were interfering with his pleasure.

With the sudden increase in volume, the sultry voice of the French chanteuse on tape turned into a well-modulated shriek to the eardrums of the brunette.

Lisle looked sideways at the woman. She was beautiful, statuesque, one of the most fetching beauties he'd encountered on the islands. But to him she was ultimately boring. She had outstayed her welcome.

Everything that could be done had been done. There was no love between them, just cash.

"If you don't like it," he said, "you can always swim to shore."

"You're insane."

He smiled at her long and lewdly. It was a smile that had often been the last thing seen by many a victim. "That's always a possibility," he agreed.

She swore at him and then grabbed her top, tugging it free from the fly bridge. Then, suddenly a modest woman, she picked up the towel she'd been lying on and wrapped it around her well-tanned and freshly lotioned body.

With the furious pace of a wronged woman, she stamped her bare feet on the hot metal deck as she sprinted down to the cabin below.

Lisle laughed, enjoying the incessantly loud music blasting by his ear and the chilled bottle of wine he fished from the bucket beside him. He tilted it to his mouth and took another long hard swallow of grape obliteration.

A jet ski whined near the boat.

Lisle turned up the cassette player to full volume, straining the small speaker with the shrill sound of the chanteuse. Her normally evocative words were nearly indecipherable and weighted down with a tinny reverb.

But at least the sound of the music from his native Paris drowned out the sound of the obnoxious jet skier who was now bearing down upon the boat.

Perhaps it was a tourist eager to sneak a peek at the siren who'd shared his bed these past two days.

Too bad, Lisle thought. The woman was gone.

And so was his patience.

The jet skier had pulled alongside the boat, cutting the throttle as he drifted closer.

The hard rubber bumper that ran alongside the edge of the high-performance water toy bumped loudly into the hull of the sport-fishing boat.

Lisle sat straight up, a deadly threat forming upon his lips.

Then he saw the man aboard the jet ski. His face was lined with years of war, and his eyes were empty of mercy. That was made clear by the Ruger Mk II .22 pistol he pointed at the Frenchman's face. It was all barrel, with a long and wicked businesslike sound suppressor attached to it.

He was wearing a black wet suit with a waterproof and bulletproof flotation vest. Whoever he was, the man had obviously come prepared for a battle.

Sidney turned down the music and stared hard at the intruder who was floating just a few yards away, one hand gripping the handlebar controls, the other holding the Ruger.

He cursed himself for being caught out in the open. But the damned machines were so common in Caribbean playgrounds that he hadn't really paid any notice to it.

The jet ski was one of the latest models, with a streamlined front end, wide-cushioned seat and high-performance engine. The driver could sit back for the long haul in pure comfort or stand on the runners while working the high-powered throttle.

The man on the floating motorcycle gestured sharply with the silenced pistol.

"What do you want?" Lisle asked, carefully enunciating his words to erase any trace of his French accent. "Who do you think you are, coming out here and threatening an innocent man?"

"Innocent?"

"I'm here on a vacation," Lisle said, continuing the bluff. "Me and my...fiancée are here for—"

"Your 'fiancée' is a pro. For that matter, so are you. Different profession, though. In a way."

Though the insult obviously stung him, Lisle tried to ignore it and shook his head sadly like a frightened and bewildered civilian facing a madman. "You must have mistaken me for someone else. I really don't know what you are talking about—I give you my word."

"That's not giving a hell of a lot," Bolan said.

"Please," he pleaded, still feigning his innocence, "just listen to me. If you'll come on board, I'm sure we can work this out to everyone's satisfaction."

"Not unless you plan on putting a bullet to your head. Game's over, Sidney."

At the sound of his name, the Frenchman looked up in surprise. "Ah. So you do know me. Very well. My offer still holds. Come on board and we'll discuss the matter like gentlemen. After all, we are in the same business."

Bolan glanced past him toward the cabin. He didn't want the woman to come back on deck and walk into the middle of a firefight. And he couldn't just kill Sidney Lisle.

He wanted to keep Carib Command in the dark as long as possible about what was happening to its gunmen. Let the woman think Lisle had deserted her in the middle of the bay. Such unchivalrous behavior was a distinct possibility with the man she kept company with. After watching the two of them through his field glasses for the past half hour, it was plain they were no longer bosom pals.

"Actually," Bolan said, "I'm here to put you out of business. Unless you climb aboard and tell me everything you know about Carib Command."

"There's not much to tell," Lisle replied. "It's just a temporary thing. I'm providing security for some island businessmen."

"A bit more than that, isn't it?"

"What do you mean?"

"I saw the tape, Sidney."

"What tape?"

"Of the massacre. There were survivors—"

The Frenchman moved suddenly, rolling over and grabbing for the holster hidden beneath a pile of towels and a shirt. He'd been edging closer to it all along.

Bolan squeezed the trigger of the Ruger Mk II just as the Carib Command assassin cleared a heavy automatic from his holster. The cough of the silenced .22

was a bit louder than the smack of the slug into the Frenchman's shoulder.

The deadly lightweight weapon coughed again immediately after the first shot, sending another round into the meaty part of Lisle's forearm.

The heavy automatic dropped onto the curved foredeck with a loud clattering thunk and skidded into the water. And Sidney Lisle dropped over the side of the boat with a third round embedded in his skull.

As soon as the assassin splashed into the water, Bolan pulled open the waterproof compartment, dropped the Ruger .22 inside, then gripped the steering bar and gave it full throttle.

The jet ski spun in a sharp, controlled turn, creating a huge wake in its path as Bolan gunned it over to the other side of the boat.

He reached down for the Frenchman's floating body and pulled it out of the water, draping it over the back of the cushion seat as he headed out to deeper water.

The woman would be all right, Bolan reflected. If she couldn't pilot the boat back to shore, she could probably work the radio to call for help. If all else failed, she could always wave her bikini top as a distress signal that would surely be answered by some of the yachtsmen in the area.

Whatever happened, she was better off without having Sidney Lisle aboard.

TRAVIS LATHROP WALKED slowly along the two-lane road that connected Cape Brethren's string of beachside hotels, restaurants and rustic-roofed, open-air boutiques.

Some stretches of beach were wall-to-wall sunbathers. Some were more sparsely populated, with a few isolated souls baking in the sun or lolling under beach umbrellas.

The sound of waves crashing on the shore and the soft laughter of lovers cavorting on the sand drifted up to him—and through him.

Lathrop was lost in thought, lost in drink. Maybe just plain lost.

He was barely cognizant of the dry blanket of heat beating down on the back of his neck and blistering his exposed skin. And the parched sensation in his throat had been there for so long it almost seemed normal.

He'd been walking for hours in a luckless effort to run away from himself.

The gray-bearded mercenary had tried drinking away the memory of the massacre in the jungle, but it always came back to him, as fresh in his mind as the pleas of the girl lying on the ground before him...the girl whose terrified face looked up at him as if he was some kind of barely human monster.

He wondered if she lived after all. Maybe the shock had killed her. Maybe one of the others had gone back and finished her off when he wasn't looking.

The newspapers hadn't mentioned all the names of the dead, and the government had thrown a security blanket around the area, protecting it with armed guards from any more looters.

But the protection was too late.

Carib Command looters had already taken their fair share of plunder and placed it on the underground market in antiquities. It wasn't the looting that bothered him—he'd been on similar jaunts before. Many times the looting expeditions were indirectly sponsored by museums. More often they were backed by individual collectors or brokers who knew how to disguise their provenance once the mercenaries came back with the goods.

But that kind of plunder was legitimate in his eyes. After all, those relics were forgotten treasures waiting to be unearthed, precious gifts left over from ancestors. What good were gifts if they weren't taken by those who found them?

But murdering all those people in order to get at that fortune was too much, even for a man like Lathrop, who'd seen his fair share of brutality in the merc world.

And when the leaders of the cartel dressed up the action with propaganda—claiming it was a pitched battle between Carib Command patriots and imperialist government forces—Lathrop felt as if he'd signed up for a tour with Orwellian storm troopers.

He wanted out.

But Parker held his passport. And worse, the higher-ups in the cartel held his fate in their hands. If Lathrop made a run for it and managed to get off the island, they would send hit teams after him.

Or maybe they would just broadcast the information that he was involved in the massacre—maybe even blame it on him—and the U.S. government would send *their* people after him.

It was a no-win situation, he thought as he trudged along the sunbaked shoulder of the road.

It got worse one minute later when a battered gray utility van slowly veered off the road and cruised alongside him. The van came so close that he had to jump back out of the way to keep from getting hit.

At the same time a couple who'd been walking toward him from the opposite direction suddenly picked up their pace. Until just a moment ago the scruffy-looking tattooed guy in jeans and faded T-shirt had his arm around the girl's shoulder.

But while Lathrop's attention was diverted by the van, the man's arm dropped down. He was holding an M-11 machine pistol in his hand.

At about 1200 rounds per minute, Lathrop had about twenty seconds before he caught a full clip in the gut.

The girl was armed with a smile, soul-shredding eyes and an automatic pistol. "Hi," she said as if Lathrop was a long-lost friend. "How are you doing?"

While he was disoriented by the incongruous approach of the murderous couple, the sliding door on the van rolled wide open. Inside was a man in black, sitting on a bench pointing a Beretta at him.

Another man inside the van cocked a pump-action shotgun, creating a sound that froze Lathrop in place. Even though he knew it was a psychological technique intended for show, the wielder of the shotgun had achieved the desired effect.

The entire maneuver happened with split-second timing. One moment he was walking along the road, and the next moment he was facing a special-ops unit. The slick part about it was that nothing seemed out of the ordinary.

None of the operators who sprung the trap seemed tense, and their voices stayed calm and matter-of-fact. If anyone from the beach saw them, they wouldn't give it a second thought.

Having been on a few such operations himself and sensing there was still another unit in the field, Lathrop slowly turned his head.

And there he saw the third part of the pincer team. A taxicab had pulled up quietly behind him, and the driver was standing beside the door with a revolver in his hand.

"Get in, Travis," the man with the Beretta ordered, his commanding voice pulling Lathrop's gaze back to the van.

The merc forced himself to stay calm, keeping his hands still as he focused on the man in black, the craggy-faced warrior who was running the show.

"If I get in, you'll kill me."

"If I wanted to kill you, you'd be dead already. Here and now. It happens where it happens. I'm not particular."

"What do you want from me?"

"Get in and we'll talk about it."

Lathrop hesitated, thinking for a moment that if he had to die, this was as good a place as any.

"I'm giving you a chance," the man in black growled. "I don't like doing it, but I can make a deal with you."

There was something in the man's eyes and his even tone of voice that convinced Lathrop he was telling the truth. But he still was wary. He'd seen enough apparently solid deals suddenly go down in flames because of interference from the local powers. "We're on foreign soil," he said. "What gives you the authority to make a deal here?"

"I'm taking the authority."

Lathrop nodded. "Then I'm taking the deal." If nothing else, it was postponing death for a while. He climbed into the van and sat across from the man in black.

"Here's the rules, Travis. Play it straight with me, and this can be your ride out of here. Cross me, and this is your last ride, period. Got it?"

Lathrop nodded.

As the van drove away, the man in black filled the merc in on the videotape they had of the massacre, tape that showed he wasn't involved in the killing. And they also had testimony from the girl that he'd helped her slip away from the massacre.

"She's still alive?"

Bolan studied the man, saw it was important to him, then nodded. "Yeah, she's still alive. The question is, are you going to stay alive?"

"I'm planning on it. I mean, that's part of the deal, isn't it?"

"Yeah, it is. If you give us something we can use. So far, we've offered the same deal to four other men who were on that raid. But they couldn't—or wouldn't—lead us to the people we want to get."

"What happened to them?"

"They're no longer with us."

Lathrop leaned back against the side of the van as it accelerated uphill. They were taking him outside of the city. A safehouse probably. "Tell me what you want," he said, "and I'll tell you what I can."

"I want to take out Dedrick Cambruna."

Lathrop was about to tell the man it was a waste of time. Too many others had tried to get Cambruna. But there was something about the man sitting across from him, something emanating from him that made him think perhaps it finally was possible.

It was more than just the man's incredible physical strength and control of his emotions. He could see that the man was in peak condition and moved and spoke with total confidence. But there was also mental conditioning at work in this man. He was totally focused on his goal of ridding the world of Cambruna—and he would burn through anything in his way like a heat-seeking missile.

So Lathrop kept silent and listened to the man make his other demands.

"I want the hierarchy of Carib Command. I want Gordon Parker, and I want the names of anyone in the ISF or in government office who is collaborating with Cambruna. Can you help me?"

"Yeah, I can help," Lathrop said, thinking of how Parker had engineered the massacre. "It'll be a pleasure."

"Start with Cambruna."

"I'm not sure if I can give you him. But I can tell you some of the places he and his lieutenants use. Especially a place in Silver Bay, a resort he's got his hooks into."

"How do you know about it?"

"I worked a lot of security details, bodyguarding the big shots in the organization as they moved around from place to place. Parker would parcel our unit out like we were some kind of lottery prize."

"And Parker?"

"Parker is a creature of habit," Lathrop replied. "Or maybe just a creature. We'll get him."

Now that he'd committed himself to the other side, Lathrop continued the briefing in a rapid-fire patter, outlining every detail he knew about the Carib Command operation.

When he started talking about the number of people working for the organization, his questioner leaned forward on the bench. His eyes had a hard and machinelike cast, like a man calculating the odds.

"You've got a military background," Bolan said. "Seen a lot of action. How do you rate Carib Command troops?"

"A lot of stone killers found their lot in life working for those guys," Lathrop replied. "Then there's the professionals, mostly soldiers recruited from the island forces, and mercs like me who hire on for a bit of freelance soldiering." He revealed the presence of a special team of mercs kept isolated from everyone else and based on one of the outer islands.

"We know," Bolan told him. "ISF is keeping an eye on them. But how do you know about them?"

Lathrop smiled. "I was there when Parker was selecting the team. Hell, he ran some of the teams by me for my opinion. We got along great when I first signed on."

"Then what happened?"

"The real me came out. He didn't like that at all. Thought he was buying himself a model soldier."

After another twenty minutes of driving through the hills and going back over some of the details of Lathrop's story, the Executioner rapped on the metal door that separated them from the front of the van.

The vehicle slowed and rolled to the side of the road. When it came to a stop, the tattooed man with the M-11 slid the door open, joining Bolan and the shotgunner who'd been keeping a hawk eye on Lathrop.

"This man will take over from here on in," Bolan said. "He'll debrief you. He'll protect you."

"But you gave your word—"

The Executioner reached over and gripped Lathrop on the shoulder. "I did. And it's good with these people. Talk to them like you talk to me, and you got nothing to worry about." He slid out through the door behind him, stepped onto the roadside and climbed into the special-ops taxicab that had followed the van.

ON THE WAY BACK to his hotel, Bolan had the taxi driver pull over near one of the phone booths near the Cape Brethren boardwalk. He dialed a number that immediately connected him to one of Colonel Mantrell's secure cutout lines and left a message in code that he wanted to set up a meet.

He had information to share, but not the informant. Since the ISF still seemed vulnerable to penetration, Bolan would keep Travis Lathrop in care of his contact agent.

Together they would keep the pressure on Carib Command.

7

Dedrick Cambruna stood as still as a masthead on the rosewood foredeck of the 110-foot yacht floating in the still blue waters of the sheltered cove.

His feet were planted firmly on the deck, and his hands were clasped solemnly in front of him like a statesman contemplating the problems of the world.

As the thick clouds shifted overhead to once again expose the sun, his long fingers curled over his forehead to protect his light copper skin from the harsh, fiery rays.

He continued to look inland at the distant white columns of Government House.

Other yachts and pleasure boats cruised slowly through the bay, pausing long enough for a good look at the fabled seat of government. It was a must-see on any visitor's list.

But Cambruna wanted to do a lot more than visit Government House. He wanted to occupy it.

It had become an obsession with the acknowledged senior member of Carib Command.

At least once a day the silver-haired cartel chief took one of his yachts out into the bay to dream and scheme about the day he and *his* advisers would rule the country from within the genteel walls of Government House.

St. Andreas needed a strong ruler who could stamp his authority upon the islands, someone unafraid to take the drastic measures necessary to clamp down on anyone who interfered with the destiny of Carib Command.

Someone like Dedrick Cambruna.

The islander had come up the hard way, working as a fisherman with his father until he saved up enough to buy his own boat. His fishing boat had soon become a charter boat for tourists who had plenty of money to spend and endless orders to give.

When he tired of catering to the whims of the foreign and monied intruders, he'd turned the charter boat to a more profitable trade and joined the free-booting ranks of the smugglers making their fortune in the Caribbean.

He worked hard and had prospered in the dangerous trade. And anyone who crossed him or stood in his way was taken out. With his profits he had bought more cigarette boats he used for off-loading mother ships. Soon he'd had enough to buy his first freighter to ferry contraband from South America.

From then on he controlled the mother ships, enlisting smaller fish to carry out the riskier aspects of the coke-and-smoke trade.

As the money had poured in, he invested it in legitimate businesses and illegitimate politicians. At first he'd just wanted to buy protection for his activities. But his ambitions had grown along with his power.

But paying off government officials and security officers was a delicate and dangerous business, with no guarantee they wouldn't sell *him* out in order to save themselves. He had decided it was better to take over the government entirely.

Thus began his campaign to undermine the existing infrastructure and plunge the country into such chaos that only someone as powerful as Dedrick Cambruna could restore order.

His campaign had been working perfectly—until Colonel Mantrell brought in some outside help.

Word had spread quickly through the island that the outside help was the Executioner. There was no hard proof—the man was covering his tracks well. But the rising body count pointed to his presence on the island.

A presence that had to be erased.

Cambruna turned slightly as a freshly painted cabin cruiser drifted toward the yacht. Until just recently the vessel had belonged to a retired couple from Florida who'd been making a circuit of the islands.

The circuit was ended by a Carib Command boarding party that murdered the old couple and took them out into deep water. Then they weighted the bodies down and threw them over the side.

The addition to the fleet would help replace some of the boats lost in the failed ambush.

As the cabin cruiser pulled alongside, Cambruna looked down and saw a very worried Gordon Parker rapidly climbing up the ladder to the yacht, as if his speed and deference could wash away his failure.

Cambruna glanced back toward the shore, ignoring the military minion's approach.

GORDON PARKER STOPPED ten feet from the cartel leader, brought up short by the sudden appearance of the cartel leader's right-hand man, Rudy Pierce, a fellow islander who grew up in Cambruna's shadow and had lurked there ever since. A rail-thin man with an easy smile and a quick blade, Pierce patted him down for weapons.

"I left my piece down below," Parker protested. "I know the rules, Rudy. Hell, I made most of them when you brought me into the operation—"

"In better times," the man replied coldly. "You were an asset then and had our trust."

"What are you saying?" Parker demanded.

"He's saying we've fallen on hard times," Cambruna stated, still speaking with his back to the British soldier. "Or maybe it's just you who have fallen."

"Mr. Cambruna, please let me explain. I know we've had our setbacks—"

"Setbacks?" Cambruna repeated. He turned slowly, lowering his withering gaze upon the British commando.

Parker instinctively stepped back when the aging man's eyes bored into him. It wasn't fear of his physical power that made him do so. It was knowledge of what he'd done to those who betrayed or angered him in the past, abject recognition of the power the underworld statesman wielded.

Cambruna savored the fear and uncertainty that played upon the clean-shaven face of the spit-and-polish soldier he'd bought and paid for so long ago.

The head of Carib Command held his feral gaze for several more seconds, playing out the "top dog" maneuver until Parker looked away and lowered his head like a chastised schoolboy.

A dark light glinted in Cambruna's eyes as he took a few steps closer toward the man he'd summoned to his floating fortress.

"I consider it more than a setback when almost half of your *elite* squad fails to return from shore leave."

He clasped his scarred and callused hands together again in a monklike pose. Then he looked down on them like an oracle reading the future in the delicate gold-and-jeweled rings on his fingers. The future was red. Blood red.

"I'm working on locating them now," Parker said. "Several of my best men are on it."

"That might not be good enough. We must assume that several other of your best men are already dead."

"It's still too early to tell—"

"Coincidence tells us all we need to know," Cambruna said, stepping surefootedly across the deck toward the British mercenary. "If one man fails to return, then perhaps he simply wandered off. Maybe with two men we can assume the same. But when five men fail to return, there is really only one explanation. These men are no longer alive."

Parker nodded as he took a deep breath and stood erect, trying to recapture the aura of command he'd worn like a uniform since he signed on with Carib Command. "If they are dead, then I will avenge them. If not, I'll find them."

"I think not," Cambruna said. "That mission is best left to one of our other teams."

"But Mr. Cambruna, I want to make this up to you—"

"Oh, you will. Otherwise, you would be considered a liability—and you know what happens to liabilities." He looked over at his right-hand man, sharing a private joke with the bantamweight enforcer.

Pierce grinned at the Briton, as if he'd suddenly been declared fair game.

"It's clear to us that someone is hunting down the members of your unit and executing them," Cambruna said. "A man said to be the Executioner. That means they know who you are. And perhaps know what you've done—"

"You think there's a leak?" Parker asked.

"No," Cambruna said. "I think there's a tape."

Parker looked blankly at him. "Impossible. I gave orders to liquidate everyone on the dig. Men and women alike. And I made sure they were carried out. No one was left alive. We made sure of that."

"No one that you know of," Cambruna said. "But some of our friends in the ISF speak of a certain videotape made during your assault on the ruins. They speak of survivors who can prove that it was not a battle at the ruins, but an outright massacre."

"A tape?"

"That could prove damaging to our image as freedom fighters," Cambruna went on. "We are supposed to be Carib Command patriots throwing off the yoke of imperialism. Not murderers."

"If this is true, I'll get the tape. I'll get the witnesses."

Cambruna cut him off with a subtle shake of his head. "You will be more valuable as bait," he said. "If the Executioner is looking for you, then perhaps it's time we let him find you."

"A decoy operation?"

"Yes. We'll dangle a few targets in front of him. While he closes in on you and your men, we'll have some of our people close in on him. Any objections?"

"No," Parker replied with the voice of a condemned man. "It's a sound tactic."

"Don't look so worried, Parker," Cambruna said. "There is a chance you may not have to go through with this."

"What do you mean?"

"There's a lot of activity at Government House today. Our people tell us that even now Colonel Mantrell may be preparing to meet with his outside man. If that is so, some of our people will follow him to the meeting."

"I'll go," Parker said. "I can have my men ready in no time at all."

"No. You have already failed me once. From now on you can best serve me by sending your men out on the streets of Cape Brethren."

"But that's where the ISF is the strongest. It'll be like committing suicide."

"If it bothers you," Cambruna said, "we can always lend you a hand."

8

Bolan pushed himself up from the curved white slats of the deck chair, brushed the sand off of his feet and slipped on a pair of sandals.

He picked up the black canvas carryall he'd brought with him down to the hotel's cordoned-off beach. It held several glossy travel magazines he'd been studying to reinforce his cover as a travel writer—and a few magazines for the Beretta 93-R to keep him alive if that cover unraveled.

Throwing his beach towel over his shoulders, he waded through the sun-drowsed couples who basked in the early-evening sun. The air was laden with the scent of a dozen different suntan oils, as well as a touch of smoked ham from the barbecue the hotel chefs had set up outside.

A redhead in a black mesh two-piece swimsuit looked up at him as he passed, her inviting gaze making it clear to him that if he really were a travel writer, he would have a lot to write about the pleasures to be found in the Caribbean.

Another time perhaps, he thought.

He smiled at her, then continued toward the multi-tiered hotel that slanted toward the beach like a stone-and-glass pyramid temporarily housing a tourist cult of sun worshippers.

He'd chosen the hotel on the northern stretch of the Cape Brethren coast for its isolation and accommodation. Its leisurely and informal pace catered to those who wished to escape the more frenzied atmosphere of the hotels closer to the heart of the capital city.

A gulf of cool shade enveloped the Executioner when he stepped into the lobby, making him realize just how accustomed he'd grown to the dry heat outside—and how much moisture had baked off from his parched skin.

It was easy to get lulled by the heat in the tropics, mistaking the first signs of dehydration as simply a warm and lazy feeling. He stopped at the hotel shop to pick up a copy of the *Brethren Beacon,* then went up to his room on the third floor to take a quick shower and replenish his system with water.

Less than a minute after he stepped out of the shower, the phone started to ring. He finished toweling off, then grabbed the handset on the third ring.

"Mr. Belasko? This is the main desk. There is a courier here for you. Normally we would handle this for you, but he requires your personal signature."

"No problem," Bolan said. "I'll be right down."

He threw on a short-sleeve shirt, a pair of jeans and a concealment holster in the small of his back that held a Ruger Mk II.

Bolan took the stairwell instead of the elevator so he could get a better look at the courier before making his approach.

When he emerged from the doorway, the warrior saw a courier in a light gray uniform standing near the hotel desk. His back was toward Bolan, and he was looking toward the elevator.

At his side the man held a thin rectangular package. As Bolan crossed the lobby, the thought came to mind that it was either a bomb or briefing material.

But the fleeting thought vanished when he approached the desk at an angle and saw the name of the courier's company etched across the front of his uniform: Island InterMail.

It was a private company, so private that it didn't really exist and had no company headquarters. Realizing that a lot of his communications were compromised by Carib Command plants, Colonel Mantrell had set up his own courier service. Staffed by a few operatives who'd totally won his trust, the service passed communications back and forth between a select few covert operatives.

"You have a package for me?"

The courier turned in surprise, unaware of Bolan's silent approach.

"You're Michael Belasko?"

At times, Bolan thought. "Yes, I am." He reached for the thin package that was sealed with transparent tape.

He quickly scanned the package for the identifying mark he and Colonel Mantrell had agreed upon earlier, a handwritten "-30-" in the bottom corner of the package. The traditional symbol used by newspapermen to mark the end of a story was fitting for his supposed persona of a features writer for newspapers and magazines.

The return address indicated the package was from the Ministry of Tourism and Transportation.

"Sign here, Mr. Belasko," the courier said.

Bolan did as he was asked, then took the package back to his room. He sat at the small round table near the open track window that looked out at the sea and pulled out the contents.

Some of the material was genuine cultural and tourist literature that a travel writer could make use of. Paper-clipped to one of the stacks of slick brochures was a photocopy of a news article about the family inns so prevalent on the St. Andreas Islands. Written in ink on top of the article were the words "For your reference." It was signed with the single initial *C*.

As an alternative to the more expensive and exotic restaurants, the Ministry of Tourism listed a number of inns that met government standards. The article had a brief write-up on each of the inns, along with rudimentary directions.

One of the names was circled in red ink and had an arrow running to the edge of the paper. Bolan turned it over and saw a more detailed map of the inn outlined in pencil. At the bottom of the map the colonel had jotted down a time—7:15.

It looked as if the Executioner was going to dinner.

The warrior studied the map, carefully memorizing the route, then slid it back into the package.

ONE HOUR LATER Bolan was cruising along a highland road thirty miles southwest of the capital. Except for occasional stretches of road that veered inland, it had stayed close to the coastline.

As his light blue Jeep swung into a slingshot turn on the steeply inclined road, Bolan lifted his foot off the accelerator.

At the end of the heavily wooded turn, he pulled off the road onto a narrow unpaved driveway, which meandered downhill in a gentle roller-coaster pattern before curving in front of the inn that Colonel Mantrell had picked as the site of their rendezvous.

The large white-porched villa looked like a combination stagecoach stop and frontier saloon, with spindle railings and rough wooden tables set out on the veranda.

A goat wandered freely off to the side of the house near a pen, where hens and a rooster scratched the ground for feed.

Far off in the distance the sea provided the catch of the day, which was advertised on a chalkboard leaning against the porch steps.

Just as the article had promised, it looked more like a home than a restaurant.

Bolan parked the Jeep under the shade of a small cluster of trees near the exit loop of the driveway. Slinging his black Windbreaker over his shoulder, he walked up the wooden paint-worn steps.

A man who'd been watching his progress from behind a screen door stepped out onto the porch. "Welcome to my inn." He had a wrinkled face, piercing eyes and lean, muscled forearms.

Behind him stood his wife, a heavyset woman who gave testimony to the quality of her cooking.

The proprietor led Bolan toward the tables that stood beneath a canvas awning. "Come out of the sun," he said. "Sit yourself down."

When the warrior dropped into a cushioned caneback chair at the far end of the porch, the man smiled and tapped his finger on the table's wooden surface.

"Now, what can I get you?" he asked, reciting a short list of island meals. "And to wash it all down, we have Red Stripe, Corona and Beck's beer."

The thought of a chilled beer was tempting, but Bolan wanted to be alert for this meeting. With all of the security precautions they were taking today, there shouldn't be anything to worry about. But there was no sense in taking a chance.

Though he trusted Mantrell, he was still uneasy about the large number of ISF and IDF personnel whose loyalty was questionable.

"Any cold soda?" Bolan asked.

"Bottles of cola and island-brewed root beer. The real stuff. Just right for a hot day like this. You'll never forget it."

"Root beer," Bolan said.

The man nodded, then waited expectantly for the rest of his guest's order.

"That's it for now. Seems I got here a bit too early. A friend of mine is supposed to meet me here."

The man raised his eyebrows.

Bolan reached into his wallet and passed several bills to him. "That should cover your trouble."

He laughed. "And that will buy you a lot of root beer," he replied, folding the bills and tucking them into his shirt pocket.

The warrior sat at the table and waited, watching the distant road as he listened to the steel-band music that drifted from somewhere inside.

From his vantage point he had a clear view of the driveway where it first split off from the road.

After about twenty minutes Bolan saw a familiar dark gray Mercedes turn off onto the driveway and head toward the restaurant.

Up on the main road a couple of farm vehicles clattered by, followed by an old bus with bright murallike paint covering almost every inch of it.

A few moments later a red convertible roared past the driveway, giving Bolan a glimpse of a woman in the passenger seat with wild Medusa-like hair blowing in the wind.

He kept his eye on the road as the Mercedes continued bouncing down the unpaved driveway, noting the number and types of vehicles that drove past.

The Mercedes prowled slowly past the white porch before circling back and rolling to a stop behind Bolan's Jeep on a patch of faded yellow grass.

The Executioner waved the all-clear toward the tinted windows of the government car.

The back door swung open, and Mantrell stepped out from the Mercedes. He leaned his head back inside the car and spoke briefly to the driver, who kept the vehicle running like an air-conditioned cocoon as the ISF chief headed toward the steps of the inn.

He wore a light-colored suit that at first gave him the look of a country gentleman out making the rounds. But as he climbed the steps, Bolan caught a good look at the man's eyes. His somber gaze showed that the weight of war had fallen heavily upon his broad shoulders.

"Good to see you," Mantrell said, shaking the warrior's hand as he sat across from him.

"Looks like we've both got a lot of talking to do," the Executioner said.

Mantrell nodded. "Unfortunately that is so. There are several developments—" He fell silent as the innkeeper suddenly appeared beside them. With a flourish he set two fresh bottles of root beer on the tabletop. He greeted Mantrell, then stood ready to take their orders.

"Nothing just now," Bolan told him.

"I'll bring you *something*. Even now my wife is preparing an especially fine dish—"

"We're really not that hungry just yet," Mantrell said, eager to share Intel with the Executioner.

"Not hungry?"

The colonel nodded.

"This is my home," the innkeeper said, folding his arms in front of him and looking down at his two reluctant dinner guests. "It is also a fine inn. If you are not hungry, then you have come to the wrong place."

"Just bear with us a while longer," Mantrell said. "We'll talk awhile and then we'll be on our way."

The man shook his head. "That won't do. We invite you here to eat, not to talk. Besides," he said, leaning over as if he were letting them in on a great secret, "if you refuse, that good woman in there will take offense."

Bolan smiled. "We'll take you up on your offer. Bring us whatever you think best."

Satisfied at last, the innkeeper hurried back into the house.

Mantrell folded his hands in front of him and leaned across the table. "You called the meeting. You go first."

"All right. First the bad news. There's a chance you might have to use some of your influence to quiet a little matter I was involved in." He told them about the three Carib Command gunmen who had had an "accident" in their Mercury.

"You mean those men who accidentally ran into some bullets near Kittering village?"

"Yeah. That'd be the closest place. You know about it already?"

"It was big news in the village when the car washed up on the rocks," Mantrell said. "Fortunately the constable who first arrived on the scene was a good man. Officer Cavanaugh is on the best terms with us."

"Did anyone else see the wreck?"

"A few underworld types hung around when they heard about it, but Cavanaugh chased them away before they could get close. Then he notified me and held everyone off until we sent a team out there."

"Were the bodies recognizable?" Bolan asked.

"Identification pending."

"They were part of Gordon Parker's team," the warrior said. "I took out one more in the bay."

"You've been busy."

"It's going to get a lot busier. I found Travis Lathrop."

"Where?"

"Right now he's under lock and key at one of Shepard's safehouses, spilling his guts."

"I want him," Mantrell said.

"You'll get a shot at him."

"No. I mean I want him in my custody."

Bolan shrugged and soft-pedaled the issue. There was no need to antagonize his ally in the covert war. "It's out of my hands. All I wanted to do was take him down or take him away. Shepard was with me, so he's got him. You can work out the details with him."

"Shepard's been known to take his time in these matters," Mantrell stated. "The operation will be over by the time he gives anything up."

"Maybe. But the important thing isn't Lathrop. It's the information he gave us." He told Mantrell about the SeaScape resort complex in Silver Bay where the Carib Command hierarchy was often seen. "You familiar with it?"

"Everyone in the islands knows the SeaScape. It's a world-class resort that caters to celebrities and wealthy tourists who treasure their privacy above anything else."

"From what Lathrop tells me, they're as discreet as ever, but their clientele's changing. I gave it a quick look over, but to find out what's really going on I need to get inside."

"As a guest?"

"No," Bolan replied, "as a travel writer. Make use of my cover. So far, I've made a show of taking a lot of photos around the cape but haven't done any real interviews. This could boost my cover and get some information."

Mantrell sat back in his chair and stared down at the table as if it were a chessboard and he was considering his next move. "If there *is* a strong Carib Command element there, then the manager won't be receptive to any kind of journalist poking around. Even if he thinks it's only a travel writer . . ." The colonel's voice drifted off for several moments as he pondered his options.

"Unless he has no choice," the colonel continued. "The Ministry of Tourism regulates all the resorts, no matter how exclusive or private they are. It would be a simple matter to have the ministry recommend a visit from an esteemed journalist such as Michael Belasko. All part of a program to boost the tarnished image of the islands and show the world that paradise can still be found at St. Andreas."

"You think he'll buy it?" Bolan asked.

"If he refuses, it will throw suspicion on him and invite an investigation. He won't want that."

Though the manager wouldn't welcome him with open arms, at least Bolan could get on the site. The only other alternative was for the ISF to come in full force.

But that was a one-shot proposition. They might get lucky and net Carib Command higher-ups, or they might scare away the bigger fish.

"Make the arrangements and I'll go in," Bolan said.

As Mantrell began to brief Bolan on some of the ISF operations related to the Executioner's operation, the innkeeper returned with steaming plates of *cascadura* and a peppery fish broth. To counter the hot spices, he placed mangoes and sugar apples on the table.

The colonel continued his briefing over the light meal, detailing Carib Command's reaction to the strikes launched by the Carib Command and the ISF.

So far, they'd retaliated against several suspected ISF informants and were believed to have executed an undercover operative Mantrell had finally managed to place in one of their smuggling crews.

That was the closest he'd ever got to having an inside man actually working on cartel operations. But the man had failed to report in for several days running and was presumed dead, or worse. The cartel had a horrifying reputation for the methods they used to make a man talk—and to suffer.

A number of other ISF operatives were being shadowed and believed marked for execution.

Mantrell shook his head, then warned Bolan that according to their latest intelligence reports the covert war would soon move out into the open. Carib Command was getting ready to make its grab for power.

"I think it's already started, Colonel." Bolan looked toward the driveway, where a red convertible had just turned off the road.

He recognized the woman with the Medusa-like hair sitting in the passenger seat, a blond knockout with sun-bronzed skin.

They could be tourists or terrorists, Bolan thought as he looked over the driver of the convertible. He had dark navigator glasses and a darker grin. He looked too cheerful, even for a man with such a beautiful escort. As if he was trying too hard to play his role, Bolan thought.

So was the woman. She was laughing too shrilly, her girlish voice rising above the dub music playing loudly from the car radio.

Mantrell looked casually in their direction, then turned back at Bolan. Though he, too, was alert and ready for whatever came, he played the devil's advocate. "So a man and a woman decide to stop here for a bite to eat," he said. "It could be perfectly innocent. We can't go around shooting anyone who happens to go to the same place we do."

"That car was following a distance behind you when you first turned off. It seems awfully coincidental that it shows up again now."

"They could live nearby," Mantrell said. "Maybe they stopped off at home, then decided to come back here for dinner."

"Uh-huh," Bolan said. "And they could be part of a surveillance team following any car that leaves Government House. Maybe they just waited until reinforcements came."

Mantrell glanced over at the red car as it backed up and parked on the grass, front end pointing toward the inn. The man and the woman stayed in the car, talking and laughing as if they were having the time of their lives.

It was bad enough that several of Mantrell's operations had already been compromised by Carib Command infiltrators. Now it looked as though his organization was so penetrated by the opposition that he couldn't be certain if his own movements were being closely watched. It was a hard blow for any security man, let alone the man at the top.

"I don't see any reinforcements," Mantrell said.

"If they're any good, we won't see them until it's too late."

Bolan casually stood up from the table and picked up the Windbreaker that had been lying on a chair next to him. Reaching his free hand into his wallet pocket as if he were getting ready to pay the bill, he headed for the screen door and intercepted the innkeeper just as he was about to step out onto the porch.

"Could I have a word with you?" Bolan asked.

"Sure," the innkeeper replied. "Soon as I say hello to my guests out there. We seem to be having a real turnout tonight."

"That's what I wanted to talk to you about," Bolan said, gently steering the man back inside. As soon as they were in the shadows of the man's house, Bolan dropped the smile.

"What is it? What's going on?"

"There's no time to explain. Any second now we might come under attack. I suggest you and your wife go out the back way and keep on going until this is over."

"But it's—"

"It's time for you to go," the Executioner stated firmly. He adjusted the Windbreaker so that the elderly innkeeper could see the Beretta 93-R that he'd been concealing beneath it. "Just go ahead. We'll greet the guests for you."

"This shouldn't happen. Not here."

"It shouldn't happen anywhere. But it is and we got to deal with it." As he ushered the innkeeper away, Bolan kept his eye on the man and the woman, who were just now getting out of the car.

"What about my place?" the man said in an urgent whisper. "If something happens to it . . . if there really is going to be shooting, then—"

"Then Colonel Mantrell will pay for any damages. He'll also pay for your funeral if you don't get out of here in time."

The man took the hint and grabbed his wife by the arm as she headed toward them to see what was going on. With a gentle nudge, he turned her around and led her to the back door.

Bolan stepped onto the porch, hands resting on his hips and clutching his Windbreaker by his side as he surveyed the tableau opening up in front of him.

Up on the main road he could see an old farm truck just turning off the road and lurching downhill on the irregular driveway. It was one of the trucks he'd seen passing by earlier, about the same time the red convertible had first roared past.

Standing in the bed of the truck were a half-dozen men who were dressed like a construction crew. They looked too intense for a work crew just stopping to grab something to eat.

The Carib Command backup team had arrived.

The more immediate threat came from the man and woman who'd stepped out of the convertible. The loving pair was turning back to the vehicle, as if the two of them happened to forget something at the same time.

The blonde was leaning over dramatically, her short black skirt hiking up the back of her thighs as she fished for something in the back seat. The distraction might have worked on someone less experienced, but not a pair of professionals like Bolan and his ISF counterpart. Especially when they knew they were high-priority targets for Carib Command.

When the man in the shades and the blonde appeared with weapons in their hands, *they* were the ones who were surprised.

Mantrell sprang over the railing and touched down softly on the grass. He'd gone into motion, acting by reflex as soon as he sensed the trap being sprung.

The woman, who'd been assigned to take out the colonel, clutched a pistol-grip shotgun. But she held it poorly. She'd been expecting to hit a standing target, not a well-trained man who'd immediately taken evasive action.

"Get him! Take him down!" she shouted to her companion. When no help came from that quarter, she jerked hard on the trigger as she tried to track her quarry. The shotgun blast roared harmlessly overhead.

While she fired at the sky, Mantrell darted forward in a crouch and got off two 9 mm rounds at her from the short-barreled automatic that had suddenly materialized from a slim holster rig beneath his jacket.

The heavy shotgun flew in the air while the woman teetered backward, then slumped against the car. Her wild hair flooded her face in a blond halo as she leaned forward, clutching her now bloodied chest.

Then the would-be cartel killer collapsed to the ground.

As soon as the firefight had started, the Executioner reached into the concealed holster in the small of his back and pulled out the Ruger Mk II automatic pistol. Turning slightly sideways, thereby presenting less of a target, he leapt down the front steps of the inn and fired on the run.

The rounds from the Ruger climbed up the target in two-inch intervals that chopped into the driver's throat, jaw and forehead with loud, blood-bursting impact.

The three shots dropped the driver to the side of the car before he could even trigger a burst from the military-issue Heckler & Koch submachine gun in his hand.

The pilfered IDF weapon fell softly onto the car seat, unfired and as good as new.

The hardman hadn't responded to the woman's cry for help because he'd already fallen headfirst into eternity.

The farm truck was bouncing down the ruts of the driveway, the off-kilter approach spoiling what the men in the Carib Command backup team had probably considered a perfect attack.

The "construction crew" had reached for the automatic rifles and submachine guns hidden among the stack of picks and shovels leaning in one corner of the truck bed.

By the time they managed to grab their weapons, the jolting motion of the truck bounced them around as if they were riding a just-cinched bull in a rodeo.

They tried to bear down on the two targets near the inn, sweeping their weapons in wild efforts to cover the long front railings... but neither of their targets had remained close to the house.

By now Bolan and Mantrell had split up, moving out on both sides to flank the truckload of gunmen.

Automatic fire stitched the air all around the inn, smashing into the wood and chipping away at the railings. But the attack was aimless and disorganized. As the Carib Command hardmen kept on firing full-auto bursts at random, the two professionals went into action.

Bolan moved in from the left side, running low and staying out of sight until he had a clear shot at the creaking and jostling old truck.

Then he stood tall just long enough to strafe the front of the truck cab with a sustained burst from the Beretta.

In a fraction of a second the 9 mm barrage turned the windshield into a thunderstorm of breaking glass that rained on the occupants.

One of the rounds caught the driver in the head and knocked him back against the seat. As his lifeless hands flew up in the air, the suddenly unmanned steering wheel spun wildly out of control.

Bolan leapt out of the way as the truck bore down on him, spitting up chunks of grass and soil. He kept on rolling after he landed, spurred on by a short burst of gunfire that thudded into the ground behind him.

The man in the passenger side of the truck dived for the steering wheel, just as Colonel Mantrell's driver screeched across the grass in the Mercedes and slammed into the front end of the truck.

With a metal-rending crunch the reinforced battering ram that was built into the luxury car pushed the truck off to the right, where it careened out of control.

Two of the men in the back of the truck jumped or fell out of the bed, landed heavily on the ground and came up firing. Each went down with a bullet in the head, fired from behind as Colonel Mantrell made his play.

Inside the shattered truck cab the Carib Command gunman brushed glass splinters out of his face and finally managed to control the wheel.

The truck bounced away, pursued by a full clip of 9 mm rounds that Bolan slapped into the Beretta. As the bullets chipped into and through the wooden slats, one more gunman fell to the floor of the truck bed.

With a sudden burst of acceleration, the vehicle leapt forward and rolled across the relatively flat grass, then made a wide circuit toward the other side of the driveway loop.

The Mercedes barred the way, but only for a second.

As the dilapidated and battle-scarred truck bore down on Mantrell's driver, it swerved suddenly and crashed into the back of the sleek gray car.

The Mercedes spun once, then tilted on its side, with the tire on the front end spinning wildly.

From the back of the escaping truck, the two surviving gunmen laid down bursts of suppressive fire that kept Bolan and Mantrell pinned.

The truck roared up the driveway, went airborne at the top of the incline, then bounced back down onto the main road. Its smoking tires screeched on the hot tar as it sped away from the scene.

It took a couple of minutes to free Mantrell's dazed driver from the overturned Mercedes, but he wasn't seriously hurt.

The three of them surveyed the battlefield, their ears still ringing from the steady bursts of gunfire that had accompanied the chaotic attack.

Bolan looked at the stony face of Colonel Mantrell. "Next time," the warrior said, "I'll pick the restaurant."

9

Sunlight glinted off the chrome trim of the late-model cars in the hotel parking lot.

Bolan left his Jeep with the canvas sunroof under the watchful eyes of a white-and-blue uniformed security guard. The man looked crisp and professional and friendly enough for an armed man.

Exactly what you'd expect at a top-flight resort such as the SeaScape.

The Executioner walked through the oppressive wall of heat baking the tarred lot, then stepped into the cool shaded alcove of the main building of the hotel.

Surveillance monitors were tucked discreetly in the upper corners of the room, where most visitors wouldn't even notice them. But professionals would. So would potential intruders who realized this wasn't an easy nut to crack.

It was twenty degrees cooler there, a prelude to the luxurious chill that enveloped him when he stepped through the cool glass doors of the lobby.

Overhead fans dispersed the cool jets of air flowing from the air-conditioning vents, reviving visitors like himself who'd just stepped out of the sunlight.

The sweat on his white shirt evaporated, and his forehead felt cool. The sudden winterlike shock gave a psychological boost to visitors, making them equate the hotel resort with comfort and luxury and perhaps forget the high price tag that went with the package.

Off to Bolan's right was a check-in desk, where a woman in a white summer dress smiled easily at him while she handled some last-minute details for an American couple who were ending their stay.

Behind her stood an armed security man, leaning against the doorway of a connected room with a wall full of thin, tiered safe-desposit boxes.

In front of him the hotel lobby sprawled into a maze of creature comforts. Hammocks hung from the ceiling, with their occupants shielded from view by a curtain of lush tropical plants. A long mahogany bar stretched along the full length of the wall before leading to a glass-walled exit that opened onto a courtyard with a pool and tropical garden. In the distance the diamond-capped Caribbean shimmered like an exclusive backdrop to the hotel.

"Sorry to keep *you* waiting," said the woman behind the desk. She brushed her long black bangs away from her forehead and looked up at him with a mildly flirtatious gaze.

"No problem," Bolan replied, leaning slightly on the counter. "I've just been admiring the view."

"You have a reservation?" she asked.

"No. An appointment."

"Oh. Too bad." She curved her mouth into a slight frown, as if she were disappointed that he wouldn't be a guest. She leafed through a leather-bound schedule book and traced her finger over the names. "And you are?"

"Michael Belasko," he replied, "The travel writer."

"You do look well traveled," she said, raising her eyebrows in approval. Her finger came to a stop midway down the list of names in the ledger. "Ah, here you are. An appointment with the manager."

"We're doing a feature article on this place."

"Wonderful. Just make sure you spell my name right."

He smiled and looked closer at the mongrammed name tag on her dress. Gloria G.

"It's a deal, Gloria."

"I'll call his assistant down." Gloria pressed a button on the phone bank and smiled up at Bolan expectantly while she waited for a response. "Yes," she said into the phone. "The travel writer's here. For Mr. Townsend." She spoke briefly, then hung up the phone. "She'll be down in a moment, Mr. Belasko."

Bolan thanked her, then stepped back while another young couple moved forward to check in.

A minute later Mr. Townsend's assistant made her silent entrance, stepping quietly across the lobby. She wore a soft green dress that was snug on her lithe figure, and a small pearl-colored comb held her mane of long hair in place.

Her light brown skin and high cheekbones bespoke her native ancestry. The elegant islander was the perfect welcoming committee for guests of the hotel. Attractive, efficient, subtle. And apparently quite cheerful, Bolan thought as she introduced herself as Denise Pinder and flashed her bright white teeth at him.

It was the kind of smile that had stood up to some of the wealthiest and most demanding guests in the Caribbean. He imagined how quickly her smile would dissolve if she found out the real reason why he was here.

"I'm sorry Mr. Townsend can't personally show you around," she said.

"So am I," Bolan replied. "I was hoping to get his personal views on the St. Andreas *situation,* some quotes I could use in my article."

"Situation?" she repeated, the bright and cheerful light in her eyes dimming somewhat. Like most public-relations people, she would be the last one to see storm clouds on the horizon, the first to hand out an umbrella. With a slightly hurried step, she led him away from the desk.

"Yes," Bolan said, "the situation. I guess you could call it the trouble out at the ruins. The attack on civilians by members of Carib Command."

"Oh, that. Yes, well, that was a while ago, and I'm afraid it's been blown out of all proportion."

"And the other instances of unrest on the island. What could that mean for the tourism industry?"

"There *are* no troubles here at the SeaScape, Mr. Belasko," she said. "Our guests come here to get away from their troubles not run into them, and we do our best to make sure they get what they want."

"That's exactly the line I want to take for my article. I assure you I mean no offense. Since Mr. Townsend runs the premier resort on the island, I thought some comments from him would reassure those in the industry who are worried about travel to the region."

"Very well, Mr. Belasko," she said. "I'll provide you with some quotes—"

"I'm sure they would be wonderful. But I always prefer to take a firsthand approach. If I could just speak with him for a bit—"

"I'm sorry, but right now he's handling a crisis that came up."

The perfect time to see him, Bolan thought. Townsend was the number-one attraction on this tour. He wanted to see the resort manager up close to get an idea of what kind of stress he was under—and to see what he could do to add to it. If Townsend was dealing with Carib Command, Bolan might be able to work out a deal with him.

"The thing of it is," the warrior said, "the Ministry of Tourism said they arranged an interview with Mr. Townsend. They thought he would be as keen on the idea as they were. All part of a campaign to restore the people's faith in the islands. I believe they mentioned an hour of his time would be available."

"Yes. I recall making those arrangements. But you know how it is when things come up—"

"I understand," Bolan said. "Perhaps we should just call it off for now, and I'll move on to my next interview. In the meantime, I'd be grateful if you could do me a favor and call the ministry. Just explain the situation to them."

"Perhaps we could get you an audience with Mr. Townsend after all."

"Wonderful," Bolan replied, knowing he'd pushed the right button. Townsend didn't want to deal with any travel writer if he could possibly avoid it. But he obviously didn't want to arouse suspicion with the Ministry of Tourism and bring about a more detailed investigation.

That meant he had something to hide.

Travis Lathrop's intelligence was on target.

"You must realize under the circumstances Mr. Townsend can only speak to you for a very short time," the woman said. "Maybe only five minutes or so—after we come back from a brief tour."

"I appreciate the difficulties he's in. And I appreciate you going out of your way like this. Five minutes should be enough for what I have in mind."

With the bargaining settled, Denise Pinder led Bolan out to the grounds for a guided tour that was obviously designed to steer him away from some of the more sensitive areas.

The resort was like a small colony, a private village with everything it needed on the premises.

Apart from the sprawling main building, there were several separate cottages and guest houses in varying styles. Some of them were pseudorustic with big picture windows looking out at the sea. Others were peach-colored palaces with sun yellow roofs, surrounded by thick, moatlike gardens.

One U-shaped wing followed the contour of the beach where the coastline had formed a natural harbor that was lined with private docks where guests could come and go as they pleased.

That was the spot Bolan was most interested in. According to Lathrop, nearly the entire wing had been taken over by Carib Command. They'd paid Townsend well for the exclusive use of it, but now the man was paying dearly for giving in to them.

The paradise he'd spent years building was no longer his alone to rule. More and more the newcomers were laying down the law of the land.

Carib Command pleasure boats sailed in and out of the docks at all times of day or night. The exclusive resort was turning into a regular stop on the cocaine lanes.

South American freighters trolled just outside the international limits, where they were met by Carib Command off-loaders, who then brought contraband back to the island and divvied it into smaller packages for resale on the islands or transshipment up north to America.

The presence of the monied but ill-mannered cartel men was frightening away some of the other guests who suddenly decided on having a shorter stay at the Sea-Scape.

There was still a good number of well-heeled guests staying there, which made it impossible for ISF to go in there in force. Like most terrorists, the Carib Command operatives liked to hide among the civilians to cut down the chances of finding themselves in the middle of a firefight.

Several times Bolan started to wander over to the U-shaped wing, but each time found himself led away by his suddenly animated tour guide.

He used the same tactic on her as he strolled toward the wing one last time at the end of their circuit, seeking to distract her so he could get a good look.

"I'd like to come back later to take some photos to add some color to the piece," Bolan said. "Sun, sand and sin, that sort of thing."

"Sorry," Denise replied. "But there are absolutely no photos to be taken. House rules."

"That's a bit harsh, isn't it?"

"Most of our guests prefer it that way. Keeps them from showing up in the tabloids back home. If they really want to, they can make arrangements with a hotel photographer to have their pictures taken."

"I can understand why they might be camera shy," Bolan said, "but look at it from my angle. What's a travel piece without any photos?"

Denise was so caught up in the web of protest that Bolan was weaving around her that she didn't notice how close they were getting to the wing—close enough for the warrior to detect a pair of bodyguards hanging around outside the seaside rooms. They were pacing slowly back and forth along a wooden walkway that led from the rooms down to a brick-and-mortar seawall.

They weren't the type of high-class, low-profile bodyguards that were usually found around celebrity clients. These men were rougher types—strangers in this kind of paradise—who stuck out.

Though the pair tried to look as if they were just out getting some sun, they were casting hard and suspicious looks in Bolan's direction.

Bolan had seen enough. He decided to leave before they had any more reason to suspect him.

Denise was still talking about photos, promising him there was a selection of professional shots he could choose from to illustrate his article.

"That covers it, then," Bolan said.

There would be plenty of other photos coming his way.

The covert kind.

Shepard had already booked an off-island agent into the SeaScape to surreptitiously conduct a photo recon of the resort area. And there would soon be a flood of high-resolution satellite photos available to Bolan.

In his last contact with Hal Brognola, the Executioner had asked for "headline readers" to be tasked to the mission. It took a lot of pull to get the NRO to assign their Keyhole satellites to an operation, but Brognola had that kind of pull.

Along with liaising with other security forces in the region—organizing a joint Caribbean-American contingency task force—the head Fed had been working behind the scenes with his contacts in the U.S. military and Intelligence services.

At this moment KH-11 satellites were being devoted to the Carib Command operation. The multiple-lens satellites could provide real-time high-resolution photo images of the site in such detail that it was possible to read a license-plate number or a newspaper headline.

With infrared-imaging capacity and photomultiplier tubes, the Keyhole electro-optical system could work night and day to paint a three-dimensional picture of the target area.

Denise led him back inside the main building and excused herself for a few minutes while she went upstairs to the executive offices. When she returned, she looked as if she'd just done a short stint in purgatory. "Mr. Townsend agreed to see you, but it has to be short. He has a dozen other details he has to take care of."

Yeah, Bolan thought, like the care and feeding of a cartel that was taking over his resort. "I understand," he said. "There's just a few points I want to clear up."

"Just don't push him too hard," she urged as she led him upstairs to the second floor, then down a wide corridor. "He's really in the middle of a circus here. Quite on edge."

"Don't worry. I'm as tame as they come."

"Uh-huh."

The corridor led to a suite of offices at the back of the hotel. Denise took him into an outer office and reception area where three long shell-backed couches were lined up against the wall.

Above them were glass-framed posters of idyllic tropical scenes extolling the virtues of a trip to the islands to get away from it all, specifically at the Sea-Scape.

As Bolan glanced at the posters, Denise scurried to the inner office and poked her head through the door. "He's here," she said.

"Send him in!" an authoritative voice called out, sounding both cultured and irritated at the same time.

"Consider me sent," Bolan said, walking past her into Townsend's office. "Thanks. You've been a wonderful guide. Now, if you'll give me a few minutes in private with Mr. Townsend, I'll get out of your hair."

Looking genuinely happy for the first time since she'd encountered Bolan, Townsend's moderately flustered assistant nodded at both of them and quickly exited the room, closing the door behind her.

That left Bolan face-to-face with an island patriarch, a tanned and athletic-looking man in a dark blue business suit. He had immaculately groomed silver hair and the kind of predatory hawklike face that would be at home on the cover of a business magazine or a wanted poster.

Beneath the aggressively confident face, Bolan detected agitation and insecurity. Before him was a haunted man who'd made his deal with Carib Command and knew it could collapse on him at any moment.

Townsend also suspected that the man who claimed to be a travel writer might have something to do with that collapse. "What do you want from me, Mr. Belasko?"

"The truth."

"About what?"

"About what's really going on around here," the Executioner said, stepping forward so his tall, lean frame loomed over the man's desk.

"That's a rather broad statement," Townsend replied. "Why don't you see if you can get down to specifics? Like the reason you really came here."

"I came here to do a story."

Townsend shook his head slowly, then steepled his fingertips as he looked up at Bolan. "No," he said, "it's more than that. I think you came here to do a number on me."

The warrior shrugged. The man's instincts were on target. Too bad they weren't working this well when he'd first made his deal with Carib Command, Bolan thought. But those were better days back then, back when the money came in fast and all Townsend had to do was look the other way.

But now the cartel had its hooks in Townsend. Now he realized he was an owned man. The money that came in so quickly could go out just as fast if they took over his operation.

The Executioner stared down at the man, keeping him on edge and in the dark so he felt compelled to talk and take control.

"Who are you?" Townsend asked, spreading his hands out on the desk as if he was getting ready to launch himself at Bolan. "You're certainly not a travel writer."

"I do other things, but I'm in the travel business. I've got identification, bylines, the whole works."

"I'm sure you do. Your kind always has the best documentation."

"Whatever it takes to do the job right," Bolan said.

"I'm not a fool, Belasko, or whoever you really are. Out of the blue I get a request from the Ministry of Tourism to grant you an interview. The timing is more than suspicious."

"Why's that?" Bolan asked.

Townsend fell silent for a second, then said, "I hear nothing from them for ages. Then all of a sudden they twist my arm to meet with a man I never heard of. It almost seems like they're investigating something—"

"Like the sudden influx of underworld figures checking into your resort," Bolan suggested. "Pushing their weight around and practically taking the place over."

"There's nothing I can do about that," Townsend protested. "Who am I to turn guests away just because some people think they look a bit undesirable?"

"Especially when they're extremely well-paying guests," the Executioner said. "Right?"

"That's one reason," Townsend admitted. "Here's another reason for you—maybe they're the kind of people who don't use their real names. Who knows what they're capable of? And if this is the kind of place you seem to think it is, who knows what could happen to someone who starts poking around where they don't belong."

"I don't think word will get out," Bolan said. "The way I see it, you're not about to broadcast to your pals how unsafe your place is. And how you gave a guided tour to a man asking about them."

"Perhaps you are right."

"I know I am. I know all about your situation. How it started and how it's going to end. So do the people I'm working for."

"And who are *they?*"

"People who can help you," Bolan told him.

"Or hurt me."

"In a second. You're out of your league, Townsend. You get in the way and you go down."

Townsend slid his hands back across the desk, making sure he kept them on the surface when he saw Bolan's alert reaction.

Then the manager of the captive resort leaned back in his chair and folded his hands across his chest like a judge delivering his verdict. But it was a verdict against himself. "There's nothing I can do. It's too late to back out. Too dangerous to cooperate."

Seeing that his mind was made up, at least for now, Bolan handed him a blank white card with a phone number written on it.

"What's this for?"

"I don't think you really know just how rough these people are," Bolan said. "In case you find out the hard way and you need some help, call this number any time of night or day."

"I suppose travel writers never sleep."

"Someone will always be there for messages," the Executioner replied. "They can reach me or tell you where to go in case of an emergency."

Townsend studied the number, clutching the card as if it was his ticket out. But the enthusiasm quickly faded when reality set in. Going with Bolan meant going against Carib Command. He wasn't ready for that yet.

"Thanks," Townsend said, tucking the card inside his suit pocket. "But I don't plan on having any emergencies."

"Keep the number. I plan on causing them."

10

The glass-bottomed boat cruised slowly out into Silver Bay, its foaming wake marking its path from the private harbor at the SeaScape complex.

Prowling closely behind it was a thirty-nine-foot shark blue twin-hull powerboat with two Mercury 400 HP inboard engines. Looking like a rocket at rest, the high-performance craft cut through the waves at low throttle.

When the glass-bottomed skiff reached the middle of the bay it cut its engine and floated over the coral gardens that spiraled and clustered from the seabed fifty yards below.

The powerboat hung back in the distance like a floating high-tech bodyguard, watching over the skiff where Rudy Pierce held council and conducted the everyday business of Carib Command.

Eight men occupied the skiff, four on each side beneath the white canvas roof, bobbing up and down in the calm Caribbean. It had been like this for several days now.

As Dedrick Cambruna's right-hand man, Rudy Pierce was responsible for organizing the off-loading crews for the mother ships that lurked in international waters, doling out rewards and punishments, and plotting strategy for eliminating those who opposed the cartel.

A notoriously suspicious man who trusted no one, perhaps because of the huge number of enemies he'd made while clawing and scheming his way to the top, Pierce never conducted business where he thought he could be tapped.

Even though he was the man who now controlled almost every aspect of the SeaScape, which he'd already claimed as his personal fiefdom once the cartel came to power, Pierce had too much respect for modern surveillance equipment to risk holding these sessions where specialists could eavesdrop on him.

No hotel rooms.

No cars.

Just face-to-face, out in the open.

Every day Pierce would select one of the glass-bottomed boats the hotel kept for the use of their guests. After one of his men swept it for bugs, he would take some of the crew chiefs out into the bay.

Out where no one could touch him.

At least no one Pierce could see, the Executioner thought as he swam through the spiny columns of the multicolored coral garden.

His green-and-turquoise wet suit blended with the seabed, as did the sand-colored lightweight scuba gear he wore. The closed-circuit shallow-depth tank kept air bubbles from giving away his presence.

The camouflaged infiltration suit was provided by Shepard's covert network on the island. Though Colonel Mantrell's people could have also provided him with similar gear, Bolan preferred using his own contacts for the mission. Doing so eliminated the possibility of leaving behind any kind of trail that Carib Command sympathizers in the ISF could follow.

Bolan kicked his flippers, propelling himself forward along a thin, shadowy trench that led him toward the boats. His earlier underwater recons had determined the best unseen approach.

Soon the shimmering silhouettes of the two craft appeared almost above him.

Through the glass-bottomed boat he could see the hulking shadows of Rudy Pierce's crew chiefs.

Pierce was his main target. Surveillance from the Keyhole satellites and Shepard's photo-recon operative had identified the main players in the cartel. All of them were wanted by the ISF. But Pierce was especially wanted—a man in that position could help unravel the whole cartel.

But Pierce was never alone on land or out at sea. A raid on the resort might lead to casualties among the high-profile guests and celebrities, exactly what the ISF didn't need. They couldn't afford to come off as storm troopers, not if they wanted to win the hearts and minds of the islanders.

And snatching the cartel lieutenant from the midst of his enforcers didn't have a high probability of success.

That left Bolan with the option he most preferred—hitting the Carib Command head-on.

The warrior glided through a section of coral garden where the multicolored coral branches reached out like petrified arms.

He was close now, almost under the boat. If any of the men on board were sharp-eyed or curious enough, they might see some kind of movement below them.

But Bolan had already committed himself.

He thumbed the quick-release latch that dropped his weight belt. As it floated toward the seabed, the warrior knifed up toward his targets. At his present depth he could ascend as rapidly as possible without worrying about the bends.

As he swam upward his right hand was stretched overhead in a Statue of Liberty pose, carrying a radio-controlled limpet mine with a volcanic charge.

His left hand held a Heckler & Koch P-11 underwater pistol at his side. The electrically fired pistol could shoot fléchette loads in the air or underwater.

As a backup, a thin spear gun strapped to his belt held a razor-sharp bolt.

THE MAN SITTING beside Pierce saw a fluttering movement directly below him in the water. At first he thought it was one of the large groupers that were always darting in and out of the coral pathways, or maybe a brightly colored parrot fish.

But then part of his mind deciphered that the strangely colored creature swimming up toward him was a man.

And he was carrying a lethal-looking package that would seal their fate if he managed to plant it on the boat.

"Look out!" he shouted, rocketing to his feet and pointing down at the glass.

When the first man sounded the alarm, half of the cartel crew chiefs jumped to their feet, as if they'd been stung. The rest leaned forward in their seats and peered down through the glass, trying to see what the fuss was about.

"What is it? What's wrong?" Pierce shouted.

"It's a mine!" shouted the man next to him. "Look, he's got a mine."

"Take him out. Do it now, all of you. Before he gets us."

The guns came out then, but it was too late to stop the attacker from the depths.

THE EXECUTIONER RAMMED the limpet mine against the metal hull of the glass-bottomed boat, made sure that it stuck against the surface, then pushed himself away from the boat.

The choreographed motion foiled the attempts of the boat-side gunners who peered over the sides and aimed their weapons down at the water—but saw nothing to aim at.

His backward dive took him down at a slant that brought him to the front of the boat where the long curved hull made it hardest for the gunmen to get a clear shot at him.

That didn't stop them from trying.

Staggered pistol fire ripped through the water on both sides of the boat as the panicked hardmen emptied their weapons as fast as they could pull the triggers.

Then they threw themselves overboard.

One heavyset man plunged down into the water like an anchor, frantically pawing through the water as he swam toward Bolan, his white shirt billowing around him and slowing him down like a parachute.

But the man had a berserker mentality and kept on coming. He stretched out his hands in a strangling motion as he drew closer to the Executioner.

Steadying himself with a pinwheel motion of his flippers, Bolan aimed the P-11 at the man and shot him in the head.

The projectile punched a hole in his temple that let out a smokelike stream of blood.

Two other Carib Command gunmen dropped into the water and swam toward the attached limpet mine.

Bolan fired three shots that ripped through the water like miniature torpedoes. The first shot caught one of the men in the back of his neck and banged his head against the hull. He floated away like a dead fish.

The second and third shots ripped into the other man's head and hand, striking him just as he'd been about to reach the mine. The dead man floated under the bottom of the boat in a cloud of blood that wafted against the glass.

The rest of the cartel hardmen had begun their deep-sea exodus toward the thirty-nine-foot twin-hull powerboat, splashing desperately away from the smaller boat.

Bolan swam straight down to the seabed and sought cover in one of the coral-lined trenches. He pulled the slim remote-control detonator free from its Velcro harness, aimed it at the mined skiff and activated the signal that triggered the mine.

The blast lifted the skiff out of the water, practically disintegrating it in a shower of metal and glass shards that sliced the water around the fleeing cartel men.

When the debris stopped cutting through the water, Bolan swam toward the huge silhouette of the thirty-nine-footer. The three surviving members of the cartel's council were splashing their way to safety, Rudy Pierce's familiar slender form in the lead.

Bolan could almost sense the exhilaration they felt.

Any moment now they'd reach the high-speed guardian that would take them away from the predator who'd caught them out in the deeps.

Or maybe they'd figure it out before they climbed the rungs of the ladder and scrambled aboard the twin-engined rescue ship. Maybe they'd realize they were doing exactly what the Executioner wanted them to do.

But they didn't.

All three of them made it aboard.

Their immediate escape from the Executioner was also a long-range escape from the planet. Unlike the glass-bottomed boats, which were used by several of the civilian guests at the hotel, the thirty-nine-footer was used exclusively for the cartel members. Bolan had placed charges on the vessel long before it left the private dock and shadowed Pierce out into the bay.

Just as the grumbling engines roared to life, Bolan aimed the remote-control-radio unit toward the "escape" boat and triggered the next sequence.

The sleek prowler exploded in a geyser of peeling metal and flesh, the loud roar of the blast rolling across the bay in explosive testimony that the Executioner was on the warpath and taking no prisoners.

As the smoking metal rain of boat fragments hissed down into the water, Bolan swam away from the kill zone, leaving the human debris behind for their kindred scavengers attracted by the shroud of blood filtering into the sea.

11

In the main saloon of Dedrick Cambruna's yacht, the stone-faced leader of Carib Command glared impassively at the British soldier who stood before him.

Like the other hired guns in his organization, Gordon Parker had been called to Cambruna's floating command base to get instructions from the embattled cartel chief.

Cambruna had received them all like a pope or a monarch addressing his loyal subjects in private audience, urging them on to acts of glory. Perhaps to their deaths.

But his attitude toward Parker was of controlled hostility. The British mercenary who was supposed to train his troops and lead them into action had instead led Carib Command to the brink of ruin.

As Cambruna studied him with a cold gaze, Parker began to perspire. Sweat soaked through his short-sleeve khaki shirt and around the back of his collar.

So far, Cambruna hadn't said a word. But his body language spoke volumes.

As soon as Parker had been led into the room by Cambruna's newest lieutenant, an enforcer who'd just been moved up the ranks, the cartel leader had strapped on an underarm holster bearing a 9 mm Smith & Wesson automatic.

Parker stared at the holster rig worn by the white-haired warlord. He'd never seen the man armed before. In the past Cambruna had depended on the aura of menace to shield him, an aura that said he was invulnerable to attack. Anyone who went against him was as good as dead.

But that was changing now.

Right now he looked like a man under siege, prepared to cut his losses or make whatever sacrifice he felt necessary. And Gordon Parker was one of the chief sacrifices.

Cambruna patted the holstered Smith & Wesson. "You don't approve?"

"No," Parker said. "It's not that. I'm just surprised."

"Not as surprised as I am. Perhaps you're thinking it isn't very seemly for a man in my position to have to rely on such a weapon."

Parker stood silent, aware that the wrong response might lead him to use that weapon.

"Years have passed since I felt compelled to personally take up arms against my enemies," Cambruna said. He spoke with a measured and reasonable tone, like a man giving a history lesson to a slow student. "Until now that has been the responsibility of my subordinates. The ones who are paid to take the risks, to take lives for the cause of Carib Command."

Despite all the talk of the glories of Carib Command it was a fact of life that money was the main motivator for the troops who signed on with the cartel.

But Parker kept his cynicism in check, playing the good student. If he made it through whatever test Cambruna had in mind, he'd get a lot more than a passing grade. He'd get life itself.

"All that has changed now," Cambruna went on. "In the past few hours everything I have been building for, planning for, has gone up in flames—along with my good friend, Mr. Pierce."

Word of Pierce's death had spread through the island. Within hours Carib Command knew what happened and who had carried out the hit. The signature of the Executioner was written all over the operation.

"I spoke to you before of this man the ISF has brought in to fight against us," Cambruna said. "The Executioner. He's certainly living up to his reputation. And unless we respond in kind, there won't be enough of us left to take over the reins of government."

Cambruna sat back on the soft cushion of the couch and looked up at Parker. "Our armed response begins this very day. We have determined a number of targets who have helped the ISF or are crucial to their effort. Once we are rid of them, the battle can begin in earnest."

"My people are ready," Parker said. "Just tell me what you want them to do."

"I've already told you," Cambruna said, a soft undercurrent of menace creeping into his voice. "I want you to set a trap for the Executioner."

"We've been making ourselves visible all across the island, but—"

"But not visible enough. I can understand why a man such as yourself is reluctant to boldly advertise your presence to a man such as the Executioner."

"I have always accompanied my men—"

Cambruna waved away the soldier's protest. "Whatever the reason, he has not taken the bait. So now we must make it a bit easier for him. Use your man Raffell. Thanks to the videotape that has compromised your mission, he is as well-known to the other side as you are.''

"Consider it done.''

"I considered it done last time, and yet here we are once again, still losing our best people all because of one man. This time draw him out. Even if you have to parade Raffell stark naked up and down the Cape Brethren strip.''

"As you command," Parker said, playing up to the megalomania of the cartel leader.

Cambruna smiled and nodded toward Parker like a king to a court jester. "Take him down, and the slate is clean. And you will be a rich man, entitled to the same reward I have offered to everyone else.

"But for you there is something more," the cartel chief continued. "This time around, if you do not get the Executioner, then there will be a reward out for you.''

AT 4:45 p.m. the cool remnants of a brief tropical storm swept across the islands. It had come up suddenly and drenched St. Andreas with moving curtains of rain that washed away the hazy blanket of humidity that had been hovering over the Caribbean.

Moisture-laden breezes drifted through the open windows of the small travel agency that had been set up a year ago on the northern shore of the cape.

Though it occasionally made arrangements for some genuine clients, the agency specialized in handling logistics for CIA-DEA operatives coming into the island, like the "tourist" who'd been brought in by Mark Shepard for the unsanctioned photo shoot at the Sea-Scape resort.

The small station had only a handful of operatives working there at any given time, just enough to keep up its cover as a legitimate operation or offer backup to any of Shepard's operations.

A few minutes before five o'clock, Samantha Bourne left the office and stepped out onto the sidewalk, savoring the sea breeze. This was one of those days that made it a pleasure to be stationed in the islands.

She was looking up at the sky and the heavy clouds overhead, black umbrella poised to be opened if rain came down again, when a battered blue pickup truck rounded the corner from her left. It was moving too fast for her to see the face staring at her from the open passenger window, too fast to see the barrel emerging in his hands.

But she sensed the danger from the high-speed vehicle and stepped back toward the door of the travel agency.

Automatic gunfire thudded into the back of her bright summer dress and tumbled her forward against the building. Another burst erupted from the pickup truck, striking her as her body spun, stitching her from thigh to neck.

She landed in a sitting position, still clutching her umbrella.

From inside the building came loud screams and shuffling sounds as the rest of the team realized they were under attack.

One of the men, a balding and bearded blue-jeaned operative, ran out into the street and aimed a Colt automatic at the fleeing truck.

The second part of the attack team went into action. A carload of gunners whipped around the corner, firing from front and back windows at the bearded man.

The first volley blew apart his right hand, sending the automatic spinning free onto the sidewalk. The second and third volleys ripped him up and down, toppling him over the outstretched legs of the dead woman on the sidewalk.

As his blood fountained onto the street, the pickup rejoined the assault.

Both vehicles strafed the face of the covert travel agency, transforming the pastel-colored building into a ruin of war. Bullets chewed through the walls and the windows, raining plaster and glass onto the occupants. The steady fire prohibited any chance of effective response from the two men left inside the building.

They dived to the floor, fired a few shots from their automatics, then waited for the barrage to end.

With a sudden screech of tires the carload of hit men and the assassin in the pickup hurtled away from the bullet-riddled building.

Carib Command's offensive had begun.

DUSK FELL on Kittering village just as Officer Malcolm Cavanaugh finished making his rounds of the small fishing community on the southeastern coast of St. Andreas.

The broad-shouldered white-shirted watchman had become a living landmark on this part of the island, as much of an institution as the police station where he spent most of his time these days. He was the one who kept it quiet and orderly, much as his father had done before him.

For as long as most people in the village could remember, there had always been a Cavanaugh on duty. The pride and practice of law enforcement passed on from father to son along with the imposing physique.

Cavanaugh and his wife were doing their best to maintain the tradition. So far, they had two daughters and were still hoping for a son.

Lately Cavanaugh had been working alone at the understaffed police station, on duty or on call most of the time. The bunk in the back office was getting a lot of use.

While the village had grown somewhat over the years, the small police station was pretty much the same—a whitewashed cottage with a long rectangular window that looked out on the road that ran parallel to the sea.

But it was the heart of the village.

From this small mailbox-shaped building, Officer Malcolm Cavanaugh kept the peace, gave directions to tourists and advice to the villagers who looked up at him as a man who knew the right way of doing things.

He was also a voice of calm eagerly listened for on ship-to-shore radio whenever overconfident seamen found themselves at the mercy of the reefs that bracketed the point. He could talk them safely into the docks or direct them to the next safe harbor.

Cavanaugh had also proved instrumental in driving off several would-be Carib Command hirelings who'd tried to make the small fishing village one of their bases.

His latest run-in with them was still the talk of the village. When a small group of cartel hangers-on had come snooping around the car wreck that washed up on the shore—trying to claim the bodies of their friends—Cavanaugh offered to reunite them underwater. They tried to tough it out, but he'd chased them away until the ISF units arrived on the scene.

Cavanaugh's loathing of anyone connected to Carib Command was based on personal reasons.

When Carib Command was first making its move across the island, it had concentrated on small villages, seeking down-on-their-luck islanders who could be enticed and eventually entrapped.

The terrorists used a scattergun approach, promising anything to anybody just to get a foothold for the cartel.

They'd gotten to his assistant Austin Becket, a promising young officer Cavanaugh had personally trained and had high hopes for. But Becket had higher hopes and quit his job.

Hypnotized by the fast cars, fast women and easy money that came to members of Carib Command, Becket had decided to make a quick fortune in the drug trade.

He'd seen up close how they lived and how easy it was for them to get away with their crimes. So when they had made him an offer, he'd taken it.

They'd sent him on a run to Miami. It was only supposed to be a small trial run, bodyguarding some white gold the cartel wanted to unload on a new market they were developing.

But the outfit that already controlled the market had other ideas and came down heavy on the Carib team.

Becket had come home in a box.

Since Becket's death, Cavanaugh had spent a lot of his time thinking about the younger man, wondering if there was something he could have done or said that might have changed things.

But there wasn't really.

You either went through life the right way or the wrong way and paid the consequences. Becket had paid.

Cavanaugh was still paying. Every time someone came through the door, he half expected to see Becket's boyish, cocky face looking back at him, the face of a man who wanted to take on the world.

Carib Command had taken that face and turned it into a death mask, which was what Malcolm Cavanaugh saw whenever he had too much time on his hands.

Like now.

At night the village settled down and so did the station.

Until a replacement could be trained and sent out to Kittering village, Cavanaugh was spending most of his time at the station on duty or on call, listening to the radio to chase the ghosts away.

Cavanaugh was listening to Brazilian music from a radio station that drifted in from the South American mainland when he heard the sound.

It was unintelligible at first, then it became clear that it was a female's voice. He couldn't recognize the voice, but he could recognize the current of fear behind it.

A young woman was screaming, running down the beach, feet skidding on the cold sand, running for dear life for the safe bright lights of the police station.

Cavanaugh got to his feet, slid on his shoulder holster, then burst out the front door of the station with the speed of a man half his weight.

Then he saw her thin shadow up the beach, staggering toward him. As she came into the halo of light that surrounded the police station, Cavanaugh saw that it was Maria, one of the younger women in the village who'd moved away for a while to try her luck in the capital town. But she didn't have enough training to land the kind of job she wanted.

She called his name, saying it over and over as if it was some kind of prayer to ward off evil spirits.

"Maria," he said in a commanding, warm voice, opening his arms and softly gripping her shoulders. "Calm down and tell me what's the matter, girl."

The words tumbled out all at once in a hysterical cadence. She was saying something about a couple of men chasing her.

"Where? Where did it happen?"

She shook her head, continuing her panic-stricken rant. Though he couldn't understand her, he could tell she was deathly afraid of something.

And then in her eyes he saw that she was afraid of what was going to happen to *him*, afraid of what she'd led him to.

Cavanaugh heard the club whistling through the air. He turned just before it struck him on the back of his neck. It stunned him, but he kept on turning, reaching for his holstered revolver.

But his legs were no longer working. The shock traveled through his system, and he went down on the sand. Looking up, he saw her two Carib Command accomplices, men he'd chased away from the car wreck.

One held a club; one held a gun.

Cavanaugh's fingers closed around his revolver, but before he could remove it there was a sudden roar. A rushing sound ripped through his head as the two men faded from his vision.

12

Karen Holmes sat straight up in bed, jolted from sleep by a distant, unrecognizable sound.

It was early morning, still dark, still cold from the sea breeze wafting through the high screen windows of the villa.

She wrapped her arms around herself to fight off the chill that sprouted goose bumps on her flesh. But the cold wasn't caused by the wind. It was generated by the sound that her subconscious mind had identified moments ago and only now was close enough for her to recognize.

It was the relentless thrumming of rotors that she had heard just moments before Carib Command gunmen had slithered down ropes from the sky and slaughtered her colleagues at the ruins.

Karen rolled quickly out of bed and stepped into a pair of khaki shorts, then slipped a hooded sweatshirt over her shoulders.

Male voices sounded in the courtyard just outside her window. She recognized them as belonging to two of the guards from the American Embassy who'd been assigned to watch over her at the villa on the easternmost island in the St. Andreas chain.

But in the past she'd always heard them speak in relaxed and almost soothing tones. Everyone had done their best to keep her reassured about her safety.

It was different now. They were agitated, on guard.

Karen stood on the rattan chair next to the window and looked out onto the courtyard, which was rapidly filling. Several other men were assembling there, all of them armed.

"Oh, God," she said, looking up at the bright light of the helicopter cutting through the dark sky, "not again. Please not again. They've found me."

"Relax," one of the guards said, looking up at her window. "There's nothing to worry about. This is expected—"

"Then why are you all carrying guns?" she shouted back, trying to keep the panic out of her voice.

"Just a precaution, Miss Holmes."

She shook her head. Even in the middle of the night in the middle of a war, the plainclothes Marine was polite.

The descending light grew brighter as the down-wash from the rotors swayed the tops of the palm trees and kicked up clouds of dust in the courtyard.

The helicopter touched down gently in the yard. A few moments later a half-dozen or so dark figures jumped to the ground.

One of them was a woman.

The newcomers spoke with a few of the guards, then headed toward the main entrance of the multitiered villa. As they passed close to her window, Karen caught a glimpse of a tall man in black with a lean frame and a weathered face.

He had a side arm and a small submachine gun strapped to a harness on his chest. He seemed to be in charge of the newcomers, as well as the men already stationed at the villa.

Her initial panic faded, but she still felt uneasy at the sudden interruption.

Though it wasn't a Carib Command raid, the presence of this small group of armed men could only mean that something was in the air. She slipped on a pair of sandals, then headed out into the hallway—only to find herself looking into the bleary eyes of Alan Garney, the heavyset senior member of the house guard. He was unshaven and calm. Overly calm.

Behind him were two of the newcomers, the tall man in black and the woman—a slender brunette with sharp cheekbones and steel eyes that looked intensely at her, almost as if the other woman was memorizing Karen's features.

"What is it, Alan?" Karen asked, looking past him at the man and the woman.

"These people have to talk to you."

"It's a bit early, isn't it?" Karen said, smiling, trying to lighten up the situation.

"Better too early than too late," Garney replied. "Let's go inside and talk. There's not much time."

"Of course," she agreed, a hollow feeling in her stomach as she led them back into her suite of rooms. They gathered around a small table, where Alan made the introductions, saying the man's name was Michael Belasko.

"A pleasure to meet you, Mr. Belasko," she said, though she doubted that was his real name. Ever since she'd been rescued from the jungle where she'd wandered away from the ruins, Karen had found herself in the company of men with false names, dangerous occupations and lethal skills.

The brunette, who was introduced simply as Janet, was also made of stern stuff. She sat across from Karen with an air of calmness about her as if she'd been through several of these situations before.

"What exactly do you people want?" Karen asked.

"Same thing you do," Bolan told her. "Justice. Vengeance. Punishment for the people who murdered your colleagues."

"Can you do that?"

"I'm going to try."

"Out here?"

Bolan nodded and said, "Afraid so. We believe Carib Command will be showing up here in force."

"How could that be?" she asked.

"The cartel is making an all-out effort to get rid of you, Karen," he explained. "There's a price on your head and an army of cutthroats out to collect it."

"But they can't find me, can they? I mean not out *here*. I was told security was tight."

"It is," Garney assured her. "Among our people."

"Unfortunately the island intelligence services are riddled with informers and collaborators who watch our people," Bolan said. "With this all-out push for your hide, it's only a matter of time before someone sells you out and they find you."

"So what do we do?" Karen asked.

Bolan leaned forward, locking his gaze onto hers. "We let them find you."

"What—"

"On *our* terms," he continued.

"But if they know I'm here..."

"You won't be here," he said, turning toward the brunette. "She will. She's your replacement."

Karen nodded. Now she knew why the woman had been studying her so closely. She would mimic her to draw in the attackers. "And where will I be during all this?" she asked.

Bolan nodded toward the window that overlooked the courtyard. "The pilot will transport you out to sea, where you will rendezvous with an American cruiser."

"Then what?"

"Then you'll be taken back to the United States, where you'll be in complete safety until this is all over."

Karen looked at Garney, who sat there impassively, obviously willing to go along with the plan. "What about me? Don't I have any say in this?"

"Afraid not," Garney replied.

"Then how about you, Alan?" she said. "Don't you have any say about what happens to me? You've been in charge all along, and it worked out just fine. I feel perfectly safe with you, and I'd like to keep it that way."

Garney gently raised his hands in front of him in a soothing, hands-off gesture. "Sorry, Karen. We're tasked to this mission." Then, looking over at the man in black, he said, "But *he's* in charge of the mission."

"You'll be much safer off the island," Bolan said gently.

Karen sighed loudly as she leaned her elbows on the table, then lowered her chin onto her clasped hands. "You just don't get it," she said. "The whole reason I've gone through all this and stayed down here was to help put these people away, to testify in court—"

"There may not be any courts left to testify in," Bolan said, "the way things are going."

"Is it really that desperate?"

"Right now the cartel is launching attacks on key targets all over the islands. We've got to stop their momentum and take out some of their manpower at the same time. If we do this right, the cartel will send a lot of their top people here—and we'll make sure they'll stay here."

"What good will that do?"

"A lot. Besides demoralizing the rest of the cartel gunners, it'll mean a lot less troops we'll have to face when they make their move on the government."

"Can they really do that?" Karen asked, sinking back into her chair, suddenly feeling more tired than before. She thought the St. Andreas government was immune to attack.

"It's not a matter of can," he said. "It's a matter of when. And to tell you the truth, Miss Holmes, I appreciate what you've gone through, but we're running out of time here. You've got to go back home."

Karen shrugged. "There's really nowhere to go and no one to go to anymore. My friends—my colleagues—they were all down here." Another time tears would have come, but now she just felt a huge emptiness, a hole in her soul that would grow even wider if she walked away from this. "I want to finish the work we all started. In their memory."

"You can still do all that. But you've got to let us do our work first. When this is all over, you'll be able to come back and do yours."

Karen nodded, then pushed away from the table. There was no more point in arguing. Her fate had been decided for her. She looked across at the brunette who was replacing her. "I don't see much of a resemblance."

"I plan on using a wig," she said. "Same shade of red as your hair. It's all been taken care of."

"A wig? If they get close enough, they'll be able to tell something's wrong."

The woman looked at Bolan, who nodded back at her. "For one thing," Janet said, "the Carib Command gunman who could identify you face-to-face has already been taken care of. He won't be coming on this raid."

"You killed him?" Karen said, turning angrily to Bolan. "You killed the man who let me go? If it wasn't for him, I wouldn't be here now."

Bolan studied her for a few moments, carefully deciding how much to tell her. "No," he said. "He's not dead. He's just no longer a threat to us. Or to you.

"And don't worry about her," he continued, nodding at Janet. "If anyone gets close enough to see that she's wearing a wig, it'll be the last things he sees."

THE TRANSFORMATION of the villa into a hardsite began immediately after Karen Holmes boarded the helicopter and left the island for a safer haven.

For the rest of the morning Bolan, Shepard and the rest of his operatives reconned the approaches to the villa, figuring out the most likely avenue of attack that would be chosen by the Carib Command forces.

Then they set up several minefields and selected key ambush zones. Comm gear and observation posts were set up in the forests facing both the seaside and the mountain passes the cartel forces would have to move through.

A string of weapons caches was prepared, stretching deep into the woods in case any of the team got separated during the firefight.

Inside the villa the original crew of guards from the embassy maintained their poses as well-heeled guests savoring the joys of the tropical retreat. But there was never a weapon far away from their hands.

Down on the beach Karen's replacement resumed her role as the last witness to the massacre to remain on the islands. Antonio Salvador, the man who had shot the video footage of the assault on the ruins, had long since departed for a low-key tour of South America. Colonel Mantrell's intelligence network had carefully leaked information to Carib Command sympathizers that Salvador was gone.

Now that same intelligence network was "leaking" the information about the location of Karen Holmes's safehouse on the easternmost island of the St. Andreas chain.

With the cartel's open reward for the killing or capture of Karen Holmes, the islands' underworld would be full of talk of sightings of the target. Mantrell's agents were working the Cape Brethren bars that served as clearinghouses for mercenaries and informers looking to buy and sell their services.

There would be several other tips coming in, but it wouldn't be long before the cartel checked out all of the spurious rumors and zeroed in on the more logical sites.

It was inevitable that Carib Command would follow the carefully laid path to Bellamy Island, a natural choice for a safehouse. Set on the easternmost curve of the island chain, Bellamy was one of the less developed islands. There were a few resorts on the north end, a lot of private villas carved out of the wilderness and a couple of small villages.

The island was reachable by charter boats, ferries, helicopters and yachts that the wealthy villa owners used to sail up and down the Caribbean from their remote home base. Bellamy was the edge of the world as far as many of the St. Andreas islanders were concerned.

And for the covert force waiting in the villa on the east coast, it could soon be the end of the world.

THE FIRST BOATS ARRIVED in the early evening, shortly after dinnertime, when the sun was still bright enough for a recon and the water was smooth.

There were two of them, well-outfitted oceangoing sport-fishing cruisers full of passengers.

At first they lingered a couple miles offshore from the safehouse, then gradually drifted inward. It was casual, nothing hurried. Now that they had a good line on their target, there was no need to rush.

Just as casually the "redhead" on shore made sure that they caught a glimpse of her on the beach. But she always stayed moving, never giving them a long look or a good shot. She was always near one or two of her guards. Though they were still in plain clothes, they made it look obvious that they were guards at the villa and not guests.

The recon team on the boats weren't the only ones looking over the opposition.

From the cool shroud of the forest, Mack Bolan scanned the horizon through the Steadyscope GS 982 binoculars. His face was streaked with camouflage, and his silhouette was masked by fronds and brush strapped to his bush hat and combat vest. Like the other men waiting in the woods, he looked like a human scarecrow, undetectable from the foliage around him.

Bolan zoomed in on the cruisers bobbing slightly on the gentle waves. The calm blue sea looked almost the same color as the sky, separated only by a faint sun-struck line on the far horizon, empty except for the cruisers drifting ever closer.

"Hell of a coincidence a couple of boats show up way out here like this," Shepard commented, positioned just a few feet away from Bolan in the hidden observation post. The covert specialist was crouched in the narrow pocket he'd dug out of the small incline they'd chosen for the site. It had a wide field of view and a lot of natural protection.

There was also plenty of IR surveillance equipment in case their vigil extended into the night.

Two other sentries were positioned farther back in the woods to prevent any unwanted surprises. The chances were low that their position was compromised, but the strict security measures were a way of life for Shepard and his men.

Bolan slowly swept the binoculars over both cruisers, scanning the decks, cockpits and fly bridge for "sport fishermen." Though they had plenty of fishing gear, they also carried a lot of weaponry with them—submachine guns, shotguns, side arms. It was a lot more than the kind of protection a genuine crew would carry for self-defense out at sea.

"They're Carib Command," Bolan said. "Looks like they've taken the bait."

"How many?" Shepard asked.

"Looks like about fifteen or twenty men altogether. Enough of them to worry about but not enough to storm the villa by themselves."

"That means the rest will probably come in by chopper or boat," Shepard said. "Or maybe they've already landed somewhere else on the island and they're making their way overland."

"Too bad they all don't come in the front door." Bolan scanned the fingers of coral reef that formed a small spiny harbor around the villa.

"We'd have one hell of a turkey shoot if they did."

The boats that came in through the pincers of the coral reefs would have to pass through a gauntlet of men armed with sniping rifles and grenade launchers. Nestled in the rocky crevices, the small team of special operatives could do a lot of damage.

The Executioner moved the long-range binoculars back toward the blue Caribbean, focusing on the faces on board the nearest cruiser. Some of them looked familiar, perhaps from the photographs or videotape he'd seen during one of his briefings with Mantrell.

These were the hard-core members of Carib Command, regular fighters for the cartel. Dedrick Cambruna was sending in some of his very best.

Bolan set down the binoculars and fished out a small hand-held keypad transceiver from the pocket of his combat vest. Linked to the command base in the villa, the lightweight unit had built-in digital speech encryption that made it nearly impossible for eavesdroppers to realize that a voice message was being transmitted, even if they were lucky enough to stumble onto the frequency.

He called in the position of the intruders to Alan Garney in the villa just to make sure that the team from the embassy was aware of the fishermen floating on the horizon.

Garney reported back that he was already watching the boats through the villa's hidden surveillance cameras, and he was also in contact with the other teams spread out through the forest. There was no sign of any other Carib Command fighters.

They would all have to wait for the main body of the gunners to arrive.

AT TWENTY MINUTES past midnight the earpiece connected to Bolan's transceiver took his attention from the horizon.

The two cruisers had left the area hours ago, giving him and the rest of Shepard's team nothing to watch but the choppy waves of a hypnotic sea.

Now Garney's voice was giving him something to watch for. "Looks like this is it," Garney said. "We've got reports of a pair of choppers coming in from the west, flying low across the mountains. Our spotters have also picked up a few more suspicious cruisers prowling around the southern shores, close enough to drop off raiding parties."

"Nothing on this side yet," Bolan reported, scanning the horizon one more time for any sign of the enemy. "We're moving back inland to the patrol base to rendezvous with the others. Between Shepard's people and your roving teams, we should have enough to cover all the approaches. We'll keep one man posted here."

"Understood. We'll maintain our position here. Let us know when you make contact."

"You'll hear it loud and clear when we do." Bolan clicked off the transceiver, then looked at Shepard.

"They're here," Bolan announced.

"Then let's go and meet them." Shepard rose slowly from the ground and carefully stretched his arms and legs to restore the circulation. "Give me a minute to set things up," he said, holding his submachine gun at his side as he quietly slid into the darkness.

A short while later he returned with the two sentries that he'd stationed in the forest. One of them dropped down into the camouflaged observation post facing the water.

The other man quietly fell in with Bolan and Shepard as they headed single file into the forest.

TWO HELICOPTERS APPEARED over the treetops, cautiously circling the miles of forest surrounding the villa. Wary of being shot down by gunners lurking behind the villa walls, they hopscotched from clearing to clearing.

Whenever the aircraft found enough of a gap in the dense forest canopy, one of the helicopters circled the area slowly with a door gunner covering the forest below, while the other hovered in a stationary mode to allow some of the cartel commandos to rappel to the ground.

Then the helicopters moved on, scouring windblown paths through the treetops from the heavy down-wash of the rotor blades. At the next drop zone they switched roles, one chopper flying in a defensive pattern while the other unloaded troops.

At each site the heavily armed Carib Command soldiers abseiled down to the ground in a matter of seconds, spreading out through the forest like airborne seeds of war.

There were nearly two dozen Carib Command hardmen on the ground by the time both of the unmarked transport helicopters had delivered their strike teams and then flown to safety outside the war zone.

Skilled pilots might have made a direct assault on the villa, going in with rockets and chain-guns blazing, but the Carib Command flyers weren't experienced in dealing with military targets. Going against civilians was one thing, but engaging a team of professionals was another.

Dedrick Cambruna had personally planned the attack, ordering the pilots to fly to the island weighted down with a small army rather than with heavy armament. The leader of the cartel figured that when the commandos from the choppers linked up with the overland team dropped off from a cartel fleet, there should be more than enough to take the villa.

THE WOODS WERE TEEMING with Carib Command kill teams. Several gunners passed less than ten feet from the Executioner totally unaware of his presence or of the two other men in Bolan's team who were playing a cat-and-mouse game with the cartel raiders.

The warrior had taken two of Shepard's men deep into the forest to observe the airborne commandos rendezvousing with the hardmen who came overland. Under the cover of the night and camouflaged with the forest greenery, Bolan and his men had become part of the forest.

Shepard was doing the same thing on the right flank. He'd taken two men with him, knifing through the trees and stopping in the shadows while the cartel men filtered past him.

Now, as the enemy force crept toward the villa and splintered off into small groups, Bolan and the covert specialists followed them.

They moved slowly and quietly, stalking in the footsteps of their prey and falling totally still whenever they sensed any nearby cartel raiders.

Though some of the more experienced commandos moved fairly well in the woods, a good number of them thrashed through the underbrush, tripping over vines and stumbling on the uneven terrain. At almost regular intervals the quiet was punctuated by sudden outbursts of swearing.

Rising up from the dark green forest floor, Bolan signaled to the pair of operatives moving off to his right. Then he gestured toward the cartel raiders he wanted to take out first—a four-man cluster that was lagging behind the others.

One of them carried a box-fed Ameli machine gun, another struggled with a backpack-sized radio, and two others were carrying satchels.

This was one of the demolition teams Bolan had seen plodding heavily through the forest, encumbered by the gear.

After the Carib Command advance guard cleared the way, the demolition team would breach the walls.

The Executioner fell in behind the quartet, moving slowly, twisting and turning gently past the creepers that clutched at his legs and ducking under and around the thorn branches that speared out in every direction.

Bolan's backup men matched his easy, irregular gait as they followed the demolition team. It was only a matter of time before the four-man squad fell far enough behind the others. They were carrying a lot of ordnance and they were struggling hard against the jungle terrain, fighting it instead of yielding to it as their pursuers were.

After trailing them for several minutes, the Executioner judged that the rest of the raiding party was far enough ahead for him to make a move. He caught the attention of the other two men, then chopped the air with his hand to signal the attack.

All three men moved quickly forward, using the heavy-footed sounds of the cartel squad to cover their own approach.

Bolan came up behind the machine gunner, a heavyset man slogging through the jungle with his mind more on his own troubles instead of the trouble he was supposed to cause at the villa. And with the 200-round machine gun slung around his shoulder, he could do a lot of damage if he ever reached there.

This man had to be the first to go, Bolan thought, and he had to be taken out with one quick and silent shot so they could move on to the other three without being detected.

In a practiced fluid motion the Executioner stepped up unnoticed behind the machine gunner. With his left hand he tugged slightly on the stock of the Ameli, pulling it back just enough to cause the man to turn his head.

At the same time Bolan's right hand swept forward to aim the silenced Beretta 93-R at the gunner's broad forehead.

The warrior fired one 9 mm round that drilled through the man's skull, tilting his head back. He grabbed the guy's shoulder, supporting him just long enough so he could take out one more man from the demolition team before the machine gunner's heavy body could crash into the brush and spook them.

As he fired another silenced round into his next target, the Carib Command's partners hurtled forward, bearing down on their targets with the thick snouts of their silenced Sterling submachine guns.

Two 3-round bursts of silenced automatic fire drilled into the satchel-carrying commandos. The hushed *phyyt-phyyt-phyyt* sounds were just slightly louder than the sound of the 9 mm slugs smacking into their bodies.

The ambushed cartel men had time enough only for a brief glimpse of their attackers before their eyes went blank and they fell into the dense, clutching bed of undergrowth.

After a quick check of all four corpses to make sure they were permanently silenced, Bolan crouched low to the ground, holding the Beretta out in front of him in case any of the other cartel gunners had heard the sounds of battle.

His teammates did the same, tracking the shadowy wilderness with their Sterling submachine guns.

But it was silent. Maybe too silent, Bolan thought. He scanned the forest with his compact Spylux night scope, picking up the thermal images of the cartel commandos whose ghostlike images haunted the woods far ahead of them.

But none of them had stopped or even turned to look back at Bolan's position. The covert raiding party was just outside hearing range, spreading out in an extended line formation as the villa drew closer.

He swept the Spylux off to his left flank, picking out the scarecrow commandos from Shepard's team. They, too, had struck against the raiders and were moving in a position parallel to the Executioner's small group.

Bolan clicked on the discreet microphone cabled to the transceiver and contacted Garney at the villa.

"Base, this is Striker," Bolan said, speaking softly into the mouthpiece. "Repeat, this is Striker, we have made contact with the enemy. Acknowledge."

Garney's encrypted voice sounded a moment later in Bolan's earpiece. "Received. Go ahead."

"We took out four of them. A demolition team with a machine gunner. There's at least one more crew carrying explosives."

"Any casualties?"

"Negative."

"Is Shepard still operational?"

"Same as us. He has made successful contact and is in pursuit. Both of our teams are moving behind the main body of the raiding party. Any sign of them yet?"

"Ground sensors have picked up movement of a small advance party around our western perimeter. But nothing's showing up on our cameras yet. Figure they'll wait for the rest of the raiders to catch up before they make their move. We have a team of marksmen covering the position."

"Tell them to get ready," Bolan said. "We're going to beat the bushes and make some noise."

Bolan harnessed the Beretta 93-R, then picked up the Ameli machine gun and checked it out.

The clear plastic at the rear of the magazine showed that the 200-round ammo box was full. In case he needed extended firepower, Bolan relieved the dead machine gunner of a second preloaded magazine box.

Except for an adjustment to the carrying sling over his shoulder, it was ready to wear and ready for war.

He scanned the area in front of him with the Spylux and picked out the largest concentration of Carib Command gunners. "Take a look," he said, pointing toward the line of cartel hitters and handing the scope to the camouflage-covered special operative next to him. "That's where we're headed. Hook up with Shepard and let him know the MG fire's coming from me."

"You want me to stay with him?"

Bolan shook his head. "Angle back toward our position. I'll try to herd some of them your way. If they turn and swarm us, you can provide some flanking fire."

"Got it," the man said, and headed off into the shadows.

The Executioner waited until enough time had passed for the messenger to link up with Shepard's team. With his left hand steadying the barrel of the Ameli machine gun, Bolan flicked off the safety.

"Let's do it," he said, stepping forward.

They moved quickly through the brush and closed the gap between them and the advancing enemy line. Bolan slowed when he reached a vine-covered mossy knoll about fifty yards behind their target.

It was slippery, but at the same time it offered a wide field of fire, enough to produce optimum effect with the Ameli troop shredder.

The Executioner balanced himself on the knoll and swept the barrel of the machine gun off to the right, letting the shoulder strap take some of the weight while he curled his finger around the trigger.

The first 5.56 mm burst chopped through the forest and knocked several men off their feet. He held the trigger for about four seconds, spitting out sixty rounds that withered the right side of the line.

While the shock of the sudden barrage was holding the enemy in its frozen grip, Bolan kept firing from the hip. He squeezed off several short bursts in quick succession, mowing down the clusters of men separated by patches of thick forest.

As soon as he completed the first firing arc from right to left, he pivoted slowly from left to right, pouring concentrated fire into the enemy line.

As death screams and confused shouts filled the air, several gunners started firing wildly, unaware of the direction the sustained fire was coming from.

Bolan used the muzzle-flashes of the gunner's panicky fire to home in on them, dropping several more. Chunks of wood and splintered bark flew in the air as the 5.56 mm rounds fell like rain onto the surprised group of raiders.

By the time they realized where the attack came from and turned to face Bolan, half of the Carib Command hardmen were dead or knocked out of action.

Seeing the bright bursts of enemy weapons bearing down on him, Bolan laid down a clothesline of buzzing lead. The full-auto barrage kicked out a blizzard of expended cartridges that finally emptied the Ameli's magazine box.

Bolan dropped to the ground and hugged the damp forest bed while he discarded the empty box.

"Over there," one of the enemy shouted.

"He's out of ammo."

"Take him! Take him!"

The voices grew louder as the Carib Command force regrouped and headed toward Bolan's position.

The sliver of moonlight provided enough illumination for Bolan to snap on the spare box and to lay the belt in the feed tray.

Though his fingers worked with an expert skill, there wasn't enough time to finish reloading before the first cartel commando reached his position, bursting through a clump of foliage with a submachine waving in the air.

The warrior's backup man took him out with a 3-round burst to the head, blindsiding him before he had a chance to realize what he'd charged into.

As the man dropped to the ground, another face appeared behind him. The cartel gunner was crouched over a submachine gun, intent on finishing off the man who'd decimated the assault team.

But upon seeing his comrade blown away, the new arrival was startled by the sudden chatter of gunfire. While he hesitated for a split second, caught by the fight-or-flight reflex, a second burst from the Sterling subgun decided his fate and knocked him backward in a mist of his own blood.

Using the crucial few seconds his backup man gave him, Bolan finished threading the ammo belt. He pushed down the feed cover and rapped it hard with his fist to lock it into place. With a quick flip of his finger, he pushed the safety into firing mode.

"Locked and loaded," Bolan said.

From his shelter behind a rotting mangrove where he could see the approaching enemy, the Executioner's backup man clued him in on their position. "We got about ten men heading toward us at seven o'clock."

The warrior nodded. Holding the barrel of the Ameli directly in front of him, he stood up just high enough to give him a clear field of fire.

The advancing cartel gunners had slowed momentarily, put off by the unexpected submachine-gun fire. But now they were on the move again and bearing down on Bolan's position, convinced they had superior numbers.

The numbers changed in a matter of seconds as the Executioner triggered a full-auto burst. After hosing the full length of the enemy line, he tracked to the right and began a methodical barrage, slowly sweeping the heavy-duty machine gun from right to left.

The chattering volley of 5.56 mm rounds scattered the attackers, dropping some of them permanently and forcing the others to run to the left.

As they fled from the steady onslaught of lead, the cartel commandos ran straight into a second ambush.

Shepard's team had angled back toward the skirmish and opened up with a point-blank broadside. The well-aimed bursts of controlled fire added several more bodies to the count.

Some of the cartel hardmen regained their senses and returned fire, blasting away at everything in their path. The wild and desperate counterattack bought them enough time to slip back out of the ambush.

As the bright bursts of flame etched through the darkness, the Carib Command force raced toward the villa to regroup with the rest of the scattered commandos.

Shepard and his men held their fire as they quietly drifted back to Bolan's position, moving away from the patch of forest the cartel gunners were still firing into.

The Executioner stepped back into the shadows and leaned against a bullet-riddled tree while he checked the transparent plastic back of the magazine box. There were about fifteen rounds left, one second's worth of ammo that might purchase a plot in eternity for a few more cartel men.

But the reliable Spanish machine gun had done its work. The commandos were scattered throughout the forest, working in small two-and three-man teams that would require more in-close and selective fire.

Bolan set the machine gun against a tree trunk with its barrel pointing skyward, then unharnessed the Beretta 93-R. With his free hand he raised the villa on the transceiver and gave Alan Garney a situation report.

The report was punctuated by sporadic bursts of gunfire as the disoriented intruders came under attack from the outposts Shepard had hidden near the villa.

Bolan got up to join the hunt.

13

Like vultures hovering above the dark sea, the black-hulled high-powered fishing boats slashed through the cresting waves, heading toward the distant villa on-shore.

A third boat had joined the two that had performed the earlier daylight recon. With heavily armed crews on all three vessels, it was a substantial mopping-up force. They could drop off some reinforcements ashore or provide a diversion for the land-based raiding party.

But to go in as an invasion force was a riskier proposition. Unfortunately for Regan D'Oro, there was little alternative left to him. Sitting at the helm of the lead ship, it was up to him to guide the boats into shore.

The land forces had met heavy opposition.

After the initial flurry of gunfire and exploding mines, the commandos had settled in for a deadly night fight. Occasional bursts of autofire echoed across the forest, then died down until the next firefight broke out.

"Look at the villa," D'Oro said, scanning the white walls of the T-shaped structure through his binoculars. "The damned thing's practically untouched."

"What do you mean 'practically'?" George Turner asked, standing beside the helmsman and focusing another pair of night-vision glasses onto the shore. "Try 'totally.' There's not a mark on it. None of our men reached there.''

Little regret sounded in his voice. Just scorn. The size of the Carib Command force had been determined by the estimate of defenders in the villa. There should have been more than enough Carib Command fighters to overwhelm them and take out the witness inside. But obviously the strength of the stronghold had been underestimated, or the capacity of the cartel commandos was overestimated.

"Maybe we should pull back," D'Oro suggested, "like the men suggested."

"Like *you* suggested ever since the firing commenced," Turner said. "The answer's still the same. We're going in."

D'Oro nodded, having anticipated the older man's response. Though it was D'Oro's boat and crew, he was no longer the captain of his fate. That course was set by Turner. As a lifelong professional soldier, this was Turner's command and he took every opportunity to remind D'Oro who was in charge.

The more experienced military man, still trim and well muscled even in his late forties, had traded in his rank with the IDF for a fortune when he defected to Cambruna's side.

In exchange for the life of privilege and luxury granted to him by the cartel leader, Turner was prepared to pay off his debt to Cambruna with his life...and with the lives of anyone who happened to be with him at the time, D'Oro thought.

D'Oro glanced around at the dour-faced men on board his boat. Many of them stared hard at the shore as bursts of gunfire ripped through the dark forest like fireflies flashing briefly before their lights were extinguished.

Some of the men held onto the rail like sailors convinced they were about to sail off the edge of the earth. Others looked down into the dark water, almost as if they were thinking of taking their chances in the sea. A few held their weapons at the ready, as if they were life preservers that just might see them through the coming battle.

And still a few others looked up at D'Oro with accusing gazes, the looks of men condemned to death for another man's foolishness.

The guilt was right on target. But D'Oro had no choice. To ignore Turner's order was to invite certain death. But if he led the attack onto the shore, there was always a slim possibility he would come out alive.

With the running lights switched off and hopefully with the defenders' attention on the men in the woods, D'Oro wanted to slip in unnoticed. If they came in fast enough, there was always a chance of catching them by surprise.

But it was a slim chance. If the defenders were prepared enough to hold off an airborne army, he had a sinking feeling they were just as ready for any threat by sea.

The original goal of the mission no longer seemed important. If the girl even was there, there was little guarantee that Carib Command still had enough firepower to get to her—or get her out of there.

D'Oro began to wonder if *anyone* was inside the villa. From the sounds of gunfire spreading out through the forest, it seemed as if all of the defenders had already left the villa and were waiting in the wilderness for the enemy, waiting to turn the dark woods into a grave-yard.

"What do we do when we get there?" D'Oro asked, glancing at Turner's impassive and rigid face. The prospect of running headfirst into a losing battle didn't seem to faze him. "That is," he added, "*if* we get there."

"Our men are dying," Turner said. "We can't leave them behind."

"What if they're already dead by the time we get there?" D'Oro asked. "Then we're just wasting more men that Cambruna could use elsewhere." He tried to shelve the growing panic, but he could no longer hide it from himself or from Turner. In his mind it was obvious they were on a one-way cruise.

Turner gave him a scornful look and said with mock politeness, "You can be sure that I'll communicate your concern to Mr. Cambruna. *And* the spirit it was given in."

"Oh, I'm sure you'll try," D'Oro said, pulling back on the throttle and slamming the huge boat between the troughs. The impact sent a shudder through the metal hull and a jolt through the crew. "Even if you have to come back from the dead to do it." He increased the speed again, sparking the other two skippers to do likewise.

The sudden acceleration caused Turner to grasp the control console to maintain his balance, eliciting a thin smile from the face of the doomed skipper.

In a matter of seconds the other two boats followed D'Oro's example, racing toward shore and cutting a huge swath through the dark Caribbean.

If this was going to be D'Oro's last ride, he was going all out.

There was only one approach to the target. With reefs scarring the sea up and down the coast, the only way to get to the villa was to slip through a small passage between arms of coral that stretched out like claws and formed a natural harbor where a couple of pleasure boats were moored.

Once past the claws, D'Oro knew there would be plenty of room to maneuver. Maybe even enough room to pull this off.

As the lead boat grew closer to the narrow opening, Turner's hand whitened on the console while the wind and sea spray sliced coldly through him.

"Slow down!" Turner shouted as they neared the jagged arms of coral reaching out to envelop them.

With his hand steady on the wheel, D'Oro savored the sight of the momentarily shaken man beside him. "We're sitting ducks if we go in slow," he said. "The only way to get through there is to go like a rocket."

Turner shouted something into his ear, but D'Oro couldn't hear him above the churning engine. Nor did he want to. He was in his element now.

With a sudden burst of speed the boat shot through the gap of coral. He cut down the throttle, spun the wheel sharply, then kicked up a huge spray of water as the boat turned sideways in the sheltered cover, followed by the other two.

A quartet of men with M-16s headed toward the front of D'Oro's boat, preparing to jump into the surf and storm the beach in front of the villa.

But before they could make the leap, a patch of forest exploded. Several muzzle-flashes scorched the night as a full-auto fusillade raked the front of D'Oro's boat.

The fire came from several well-fortified pockets in the forest that caught the disembarking team in a wicked cross fire. Two of the men fell dead in the water. The other two fell back onto the deck, staining it red with their bullet-riddled bodies.

D'Oro saw the deadly effect of the gunfire and realized that to keep going forward would result in the death of his entire crew. He slammed the boat into reverse and backed away from the shore. While his men fired into the forest, he spun the wheel sharply back to the left, then steered back toward the coral gap.

"Stop!" Turner shouted. "Head back to shore." He pounded his fist on the console and reached for D'Oro's arm, trying to pry it off the wheel.

"You're crazy!"

"And you're committing treason!" Turner shouted. "Turn this boat around if you want to live—"

The absurdity of Turner's charge brought a harsh laugh to D'Oro's lips. Here was a man who'd deserted the island's military calling *him* a traitor and telling him that if he wanted to live he had to steer a course headfirst into certain death.

D'Oro tried to yank his arm free but found himself caught in Turner's iron grip. As the rage shuddered through him like an electric current, D'Oro pushed his hand out suddenly, catching Turner in the chest and breaking the grip.

"You want to storm the beach," he shouted, "then go ahead and jump off, you crazy bastard!"

The impact knocked Turner backward. He skidded across the deck and had to grab onto the railing to keep from flying overboard. The erratic motion kept him from unholstering his weapon, but after steadying himself once again he managed to close his fingers around the butt of his revolver.

Crouching low beneath the bullets that shot out from the shore, D'Oro controlled the wheel with one hand and boosted the throttle with the other.

Turner drew his weapon. Tentatively letting go of the railing and stepping forward, he held the weapon in front of him as if it were a magnet drawn toward D'Oro's forehead. "This is your last chance," he said, shuffling closer. "I'm ordering you to—"

D'Oro jerked the wheel sharply, knocking him off-balance just as he triggered the revolver. As the loud blast scorched the sky, Turner suddenly spun as a spray of lead from the shore ripped into his head and neck.

Like a man overcome with dizziness, Turner tilted slowly before dropping to the deck in a bloody heap. He landed facefirst with his arms out in front of him.

Still moving on automatic pilot, his arms grasped at the slippery deck as he tried to crawl away.

Turner's hand shot out in one last desperate attempt to stop D'Oro, clutching his ankle and digging in with his viselike grip. But the grip broke a moment later as he died with a strangled curse on his lips.

D'Oro headed toward the gap, the other two boats following suit a moment later. They, too, had come under heavy fire from the beachfront. Instead of continuing with the suicide run, they tried to salvage what they could of their crew and boats.

"DAMMIT," Bolan said. "Missed." He'd had the helmsman in the sights of his Heckler & Koch sniper rifle an instant before he pulled the trigger. But in that time the boatman made a sharp turn, and the shots took out the gun-toting man next to him.

From his post at the edge of the forest, the Executioner swiveled the rifle on the pivots dug into the earth, trying to track his quarry. He squeezed off three more rounds.

But the helmsman was on autopilot, letting the boat fly with his instincts. All of the warrior's shots went wide of the mark. "Almost had him. He's getting away."

Zigzagging in a wild, hell-bent evasion pattern, the black-hulled boat roared away from shore. Several of the men on board held onto the railings for dear life, managing to squeeze off some full-auto bursts toward the forest.

"Don't worry," Shepard said. "He's going right where we want him." With the extended wire stock of his Heckler & Koch submachine gun pressed against his shoulder, the covert operative triggered two 3-round bursts at the fleeing boat. He was firing more for effect than any real hope of doing damage. With the boat tossing up and down in the waves, most of the subgun's fire ended up in the dark water.

A few other men from Shepard's team also fired toward the sea, moving rapidly up and down the shoreline to convince the men on board that they were facing an army on land.

They'd come back to the seaside observation post after reconning the skirmish line near the villa. Though Alan Garney's men had taken several casualties when the raiders tried to break out of the encirclement, the situation was now under control. The Carib Command cartel forces were scattered and pinned down. It was only a matter of time before they either surrendered or died.

The helicopters that had delivered the raiders were long gone, unwilling to fly back into the midst of a firefight that was obviously going against them.

That left only the seagoing force to deal with.

UNSEEN SHADOWS TOOK AIM from the coral reefs that stretched toward the narrow passageway where all three boats were headed. The snipers and grenadiers had held their fire earlier, waiting until the boats were bottled up inside the cove.

But now it was time to unload.

The first grenadier, a specialist from the embassy, tracked the lead boat as it picked up speed and plowed through the water toward the jagged exit.

As soon as it came in range, he triggered the M-203 40 mm grenade launcher. The high-explosive round struck the first boat just above the waterline and blew a hole in the bow.

A second man launched another grenade at the back of the boat, ripping through the engine and spraying flame all over the now-sinking boat.

Bits and pieces of metal pinwheeled into the air, showering the sea with hot, smoking fragments. Momentum from the speeding boat carried the flaming wreckage toward the gap, smashing it against the nearby rocks and trapping the two boats that had been closing in on it.

While the blast echoed across the water, three incandescent flares shot up from behind the walls of the villa and cast a brilliant shroud over the water.

From both sides of the coral pincers the rest of the sharpshooters opened fire, strafing the crews with automatic bursts and picking off the wheelmen.

There was little chance for the cartel fleet to return fire. One moment they were running in the darkness toward safety, and the next they were bathing in the unwanted light of artificial suns.

In a matter of seconds the trapped boats met the same fate as the first one that had been obliterated.

Airburst grenades showered upon the crumbling vessels, while high-explosive rounds punched holes in the hulls and sent them to the bottom of the cove.

When it was over, the black-clad men headed toward the villa to join in with the mopping-up operation in the woods. When it became clear to even the most stubborn raiders that the only way they were getting off the island was in chains or in body bags, they threw down their weapons.

Of the entire force that landed, there was only a handful of survivors. Only under armed guard did they make it inside the walls of the villa they had tried so hard to reach.

Since Bolan and Shepard had the most detailed knowledge of the cartel's operations, they led the interrogation of the suddenly cooperative islanders.

After an hour of picking apart their stories and deciding they were only low-ranking foot soldiers in Carib Command, Bolan handed the reins over to Alan Garney. The man from the embassy could handle the rest of the debriefing and liaison with the ISF team that was en route to Bellamy Island.

Bolan needed to grab some sleep, a rare commodity these past few days. He headed off to the villa's living quarters and found an unoccupied room with a bed.

It took only a few moments for him to go under, and it seemed as if only a few moments passed before the sun streamed into his window and awakened him.

He got up, showered and patched himself up, tending to the cuts, bruises and strained muscles that he hadn't noticed during the night fight.

After a quick breakfast he and Shepard commandeered one of the villa's pleasure boats and headed back to St. Andreas.

More traps awaited Carib Command.

After the previous night's battle, the cartel would be eager to strike back at the man who engineered their most recent defeat.

It wouldn't be long before they came looking for him again, and he wanted to make sure they could find him.

14

The distant whine of a car engine merged with the sound of the waves surging against the sandy beach, tugging Bolan from the light sleep he'd allowed himself to fall into.

He raised his head from the pillow and listened to the sound as it grew louder. His feet swept onto the bare wooden floor, damp from the constant sea breeze that filtered through the string of rental cottages that looked down on the dark and smooth Caribbean below.

The warrior stretched his arms, then clenched his fists open and shut several times to restore circulation. Then he focused on the sound of the engine as it increased in volume at the turnoff about a quarter mile away. The straining engine droned on like an irritated hornet as it made its way along the uphill stretch that led to the small coastal community where Bolan occupied one of Shepard's remote safehouses.

The cottages were well spaced and isolated from one another by small patches of forest. Each building had a long separate driveway that led to the front door, giving plenty of privacy to the occupants.

And plenty of warning.

The driveways were lined with loose gravel. Right now that gravel was crunching under the slow-moving tires of the car that started to roll down *his* driveway.

The motion of the tires triggered a small alert signal from the ground sensors buried under the gravel. Bolan turned off the beeping sound that would have awakened him if his senses hadn't already dragged him from sleep.

The Executioner grabbed the Beretta harness hanging from a chair next to the bed and strapped it over his black T-shirt. Then he glanced at the small glowing surveillance monitor that bathed the room with a soft light.

A web of cables snaked from the windows to the table where the monitor sat. It was on twenty-four hours a day, the ultimate reality TV show that fed images from night-vision-equipped cameras that covered the approaches to the cottage.

On the screen Bolan saw the ghostlike thermal image of a late-model car traveling up the driveway, headlights sweeping through the low brush.

Bolan picked up the small remote unit and pressed a button that switched to the cameras that watched the access road.

Another image filled the screen—two more cars prowling slowly on the main road. They went past the driveway, but the sudden arrival of three cars was too much of a coincidence for the Executioner.

Those cars would be back, he thought.

He checked the clip in the Beretta, holstered his Mk II Ruger and prepared to welcome his visitors.

THE DRIVER of the sleek gray sedan killed the lights and stopped the car when it was halfway down the private driveway that led to the cottage.

Like someone testing the waters, he stepped slowly onto the gravel and tried not to make a sound.

Then he headed for the darkened cottage. He hesitated by the shuttered window before moving to the front door. One hand reached for the latch, and the other dipped into his jacket pocket.

Without warning, he was pushed forward and his forehead thudded into the wooden door.

He tried to turn his head to see who did it, but he was too dazed to do anything but lean against the splintered wood.

It was an awkward angle, made more so by the cold hard metal circle of the silenced pistol suddenly pressed against the back of his neck.

"Take your hand out of the jacket, and make damned sure there's nothing in it."

"But it's me. I'm only—"

"Just do it." The barrel pressed harder against his neck for emphasis.

The man took his hand out of the jacket and held it aloft, palm outward. Then he turned around to see the penetrating gaze of the black-clad warrior.

"That's better," Bolan said, recognizing the startled face of Rolf Townsend, the manager of the SeaScape resort. But there was no trace of the aristocratic manner the warrior had encountered in the upscale offices of the SeaScape when he'd gone there to enlist his support in the fight against Carib Command.

And now that the fight had gone on without him, Townsend found himself in no-man's-land. Since the assault on Pierce and his Carib Command had occurred in Silver Bay just near the SeaScape, the manager was a logical suspect in Cambruna's eyes.

On one side was a murderous cartel intent on cutting its losses, and on the other side the Executioner was intent on cutting them down to size. Townsend didn't like either choice, but now that the walls were crumbling down around him he figured his only way out was to deal with the man in black.

"Away from the house," Bolan said, stepping back into the darkness and leading him on with a shake of the 93-R.

Townsend followed the warrior's command and stepped softly into the sand. He raised both hands in front of him, palms outward as if he could stop a bullet from slicing through him.

"Far enough," Bolan said when they moved into the shadows beneath a cluster of windblown branches. He had a good view of the approach to the cottage.

The frightened businessman looked warily around him, then up at Bolan, wondering if the man had led him to his grave.

Bolan's harsh gaze made it seem like a distinct possibility. "Now tell me what you're doing here."

"I was *told* to come out here!" he sputtered, looking like a man one step away from the asylum. "I called the number you gave me, and someone gave me directions. Don't you remember—you told me I could come to you for help."

"Yeah, but I expected you to come alone."

"I did come alone!" Townsend protested.

Bolan studied the man's reaction, seeing if he would look toward the road where he expected the Carib cavalry to come charging down. But there was no deception showing in the man. Just fear. Maybe he wasn't aware of the company that was coming.

"It's getting dangerous at my resort," Townsend reported. "The cartel people are taking over completely. There is no longer the facade of partners. They make the rules, who can come and who can go."

"That's what I tried to warn you about."

"But now it's gone too far," the manager protested. "Ever since you—I mean someone—killed Pierce, they suspect everyone. Tonight they practically killed one of my people for just walking by their rooms. They beat him and they kicked him. They wouldn't stop. They were like animals. God, the blood was all over. I dragged him away, then I heard one of them say *I* was next."

"I get the picture," Bolan said. "Unfortunately I've seen it before. Maybe if you cooperated earlier we could have done something."

"Isn't it enough that I'm here now?"

"No," Bolan replied. "As a matter of fact, it's nothing but trouble. You brought some company, whether you know it or not. Probably the very same people who were watching you at the resort."

"I saw no one."

Bolan shook his head. "I'd be surprised if you did. They're the kind of people who know how to watch you without being seen. My guess, they're still watching you—only now it's through the scope of a rifle. They either followed you out here to get rid of you or hoped you'd lead them to me."

"There's no one here."

"Sound carries far this time of night," the Executioner said. "Two cars stopped up at the main road shortly after you turned down the drive. My guess is, the people inside are working their way down here."

A DOUBLE-BARRELED FN Browning shotgun parted the tangled brush, the gun sight snagging on the green coiling vines.

The shotgunner carried his weapon loosely, paying more attention to his progress through the forest than to any of its potential inhabitants. The over-and-under 12-gauge gleamed in the moonlight, pointing in the air at a forty-five-degree angle.

Good for shooting birds, Bolan thought as he watched the staggered progress of the shotgunner. They didn't even bother to blacken the gun metal, which told the warrior about the skills they had for tracking down a man.

Bolan wasn't about to complain. With a steady gaze he followed the glinting barrel as it moved through the brush like an antenna broadcasting the man's position.

They were city killers.

Their kind was skilled at gunning down prey on sidewalks and in alleyways with double-barreled street sweepers. It didn't take a lot of marksmanship to blast apart a man who stumbled out of a bar or was caught out in the open with nowhere to move.

But this wasn't an alley, and the Executioner wasn't a mark. He was a marksman.

The wooded corridor was thick with brush that had intertwined over the years. Sprawling vines and clutching branches created a mazelike carpet that only an experienced man could travel through without making much sound.

Bolan crept softly at an angle that brought him within twenty yards of the cartel man's path.

The shotgunner moved through the brush in an imitation of stealth. He stepped forward, rustled through the forest cover in a zigzag motion and paused for a few moments as if he were listening for something.

But he wasn't hearing a thing. He was just going through the motions until it came time to pull the trigger. The shotgunner repeated the process, coming closer to Bolan in a stop-and-start motion.

When he was halfway to Bolan's position, the shotgunner suddenly lunged forward.

The warrior reacted by reflex and trained the Beretta 93-R on his enemy. He didn't want to use the silenced weapon yet. Even with the suppressed cough of the 9 mm slug the sound could be heard by the other men stalking toward the cottage.

Just as Bolan was about to fire, the shotgunner stopped his charge.

Instead of sensing Bolan, all he'd done was to tangle his feet in the clutching undergrowth. The man swore under his breath until he jerked free of the vines.

Under cover of the man's loud approach, Bolan replaced the Beretta in the Velcro harness.

Three steps away the gunner looked right at Bolan's camo-smeared face, then looked away, oblivious to the huntsman waiting for the hunter.

Bolan waited until the gunner committed himself to taking another step. Then, as the man moved forward with his shotgun barrel raised in the air, the Executioner gripped it with two hands and tugged it from his grasp.

In the split second it took the hardman to comprehend the sudden loss of his weapon, Bolan returned it to him stock first.

The heavy wooden butt rocked into the man's jaw, clinking his teeth together and tilting his head backward.

The Executioner moved in, automatically taking advantage of the opening that presented itself. His rigid right hand shot straight out in a muscle-tearing blow that cored the shotgunner's Adam's apple.

His eyes flickered as the lights went out and he tumbled backward toward the ground.

Bolan caught him by the arm, levered him slowly into the brush, then stepped away and took cover behind a thick tree dripping with tendril-like vines.

He glanced around slowly while he listened for the other would-be hunters. At least three more stalkers were heading for the cottage, while a couple of others had stayed by the cars on the main road.

There was no sign that any of the hit men had heard the commotion. They were continuing toward the cottage, the sound of their passage drowning out the insects and other nocturnal creatures moving through the forest.

The Executioner pinpointed the sounds. One of them was working his way alongside the gravel driveway, brushing against the bushes with a steady hiss.

Another of the assassins was nearing the edge of the forest closest to the cottage.

A third man was prowling in the middle of the forest, deliberately moving much slower than the others. He was either positioning himself as a strategic backup to cut off any retreat, or he was determined not to make any contact at all.

Now that he knew where each man stood, the warrior determined the order of battle. They were too far away from one another to work in concert. At least until they reached the cottage.

The Executioner had a different destination for them in mind. He cut through the forest until he came to the spot where the gravel driveway bisected the woods.

He emerged from the darkness several yards behind the Carib Command gunman who was soft-pedaling it through the grass. The man had an automatic rifle. He also had an urgent look about him, as if he were racing with his cohorts to get there and draw first blood.

Bolan fell into the easy pattern of the hit man, matching him footfall with footfall and sound for sound until he was a half-dozen paces behind.

The man stopped suddenly, and three 9 mm rounds ripped into his body, punching into the back of his skull and tracing a line downward.

He collapsed as if his knees had been cut off from under him, dead before he hit the ground.

Bolan took his place and continued walking toward the cottage. He mimicked the pace and the pattern of the man he'd just executed in case the plan had been for them to meet at the same time and launch their attack.

But he doubted these particular men were capable of any other plan but to murder and move on. They weren't the well-trained mercs or former soldiers who'd joined forces with the cartel. They were the goon squad, street-level killers who'd turned their penchant for murder into a career with Carib Command.

Now it was time for a career change.

Bolan cleared the end of the driveway and walked out into the open toward the Carib Command gunman who was standing about ten feet away from the cottage.

The other man gestured toward Bolan, thinking he was the cartel killer who was supposed to cover his flank.

The 3-round burst kicked the cartel hardman off of his feet. Somehow he managed to roll away from the spot where he fell, clutching for his dropped weapon.

The Executioner was already on him. After the first burst Bolan had closed the gap in the darkness. He lowered the Beretta and drilled the gunman with a head shot.

That left one gunman alive in the woods.

The last Carib Command hardman called out the names of his three partners. When there were no responses, he suddenly headed back the way he'd come, thrashing through the forest toward the main road, where they'd left the cars.

Bolan jogged back over to the driveway to cut him off.

Townsend stepped out of the darkness and joined him.

"Aren't you going after him?" Townsend asked, listening to the gunman's retreat. "He'll get away."

A loud burst of automatic fire sounded from the opposite side of the woods, coming from up near the road. Another burst echoed the first, catching the fleeing cartel hardman in a cross fire.

There was a scream, then silence.

A moment later Mark Shepard's voice called out to Bolan and gave him the all-clear.

The operation was over.

"Who's that?" Townsend queried, still jittery from his first exposure to a pitched battle.

"Your friends in the cartel weren't the only ones who followed you out from the SeaScape," Bolan said. "My people have been keeping an eye on you ever since we took out Pierce. Where you go, they go."

"You knew this would happen all along," Townsend accused.

"I expected it to, but I didn't know how long it would take. When you called that number, I set up shop out here, and my other people did the rest."

Townsend shook his head, as if he were waking up from a bad dream. "You used me to set it up! I could have been killed."

"Yeah," Bolan said, "but you weren't. You want to keep it that way, I suggest you cooperate with my friends up there."

"How?"

"Let's just say you're going to have a lot of new guests checking in at the SeaScape."

"What about the cartel people there?"

"They're going to be checking out soon. The hard way."

15

Pinpoint reflections of neon light flickered across the tinted lenses of the Executioner's glasses as he strolled through the Old Town district of Cape Brethren.

Crowded houses leaned against one another, separated by bars, music clubs and smoky walk-down bordellos.

Dark side streets and alleys wound down to the waterfront, many of them one-way streets for unsuspecting souls who carried too much money or too much confidence down those cobblestoned lanes.

It wasn't the safest place to walk at night for a man or woman. Despite the occasional crowds that spilled out into the streets, there wasn't much safety in numbers.

This was the quarter of town frequented by out-of-work mercenaries, boozers, brawlers and would-be war correspondents who propped their elbows against hotel bars and filed stories from a gin-fogged never-never land.

The Executioner had drifted into the urban hunting ground less than an hour earlier. In that time he'd spotted his quarry several times but never struck.

It seemed too easy, which meant it could be too dangerous to launch an attack now, before he knew what he was up against.

Edward Raffell, the Carib Command gunman and right-hand man to Gordon Parker, seemed as if he was almost deliberately showing his face around the streets of the capital, working his way through the bars, walking up and down the streets like a man who'd lost his reason.

Or a man who wanted to be caught.

Raffell's presence had been noted by ISF informants and Shepard's people on the street. Word spread quickly up the chain to Shepard, then ultimately to the Executioner.

Too much word, Bolan thought.

Normally a few call-ins could be expected from covert contacts who'd spotted a target, but this night's sightings defied the odds—especially since Raffell was the man rumored to be the orchestrator of the hits on Officer Cavanaugh and Shepard's "travel agency."

Considering the circumstances, the man was doing a bit too much advertising.

Bolan had already considered and discarded several different attack zones. Innocent people could have been hurt in an exchange of gunfire, or the sites would have made a good ambush zone for the other side.

Until now he'd played it cautious.

So had his backup team, which was discreetly patrolling the streets behind him. But now Raffell was on the move again, heading out the front doors of a closely packed bar that had several customers lined up on the outside steps.

The Carib Command gunman started to walk past a brick wall of a run-down warehouse, with plywood covering the windows and no alleys to duck into.

This was it.

Bolan waited until Raffell was halfway down the length of the warehouse, then stepped out from the cluster of bar crawlers he'd been using for cover.

The Executioner took several paces forward and whipped out the Beretta 93-R. He flicked down the forward grip and raised the barrel toward his target.

At that moment he heard the sound of a loud engine roaring in the distance, sputtering and backfiring as it grew closer. Glancing over his shoulder, he saw a dilapidated sedan racing down the street behind him.

The warrior sprinted forward, nosing the air in front of him with the Beretta. He fired a burst at Raffell, then took a hard fall on the pavement as he dived for the curb.

Several parked cars offered him some protection from the oncoming battle wagon. It had a reinforced front grille that looked like clenched chrome teeth, and a pair of khaki-shirted shotgunners rode at the front and back windows.

Shotgun blasts drowned out the sound of the engine when the battle wagon slowed as it neared the Executioner.

But Bolan had already dropped out of sight to concentrate his fire on Raffell, who was crouching in the middle of the sidewalk up ahead and firing an automatic pistol at the warrior.

The Executioner swept the street with a full-auto burst that kicked up the pavement at Raffell's feet, then climbed up and riddled his chest.

The 9 mm rounds turned him around and knocked him facefirst to the ground, sending his dead body surfing across the sidewalk.

Bolan moved forward, changing clips on the run, and took cover behind the next parked car in line.

Another barrage of shotgun blasts rocketed into the fading brick wall of the warehouse, showering the street with rubble. A row of gaping holes was punched into the wall as the battle wagon rolled down the street parallel to Bolan's position.

With a sudden surge of power it angled toward the parked cars, then screeched to a stop.

The door behind the driver burst open, and the familiar form of Gordon Parker stepped onto the street, wielding a pump-action shotgun. Both doors on the other side of the car opened a moment later, adding two more gunners to the kill team.

The three men aimed their weapons and converged on the spot where Bolan had first sought shelter.

Like a man rising from the grave, the warrior scrambled to his feet a car-length away, shaking off the powdery debris that had fallen on him from the crumbling brick wall.

He triggered a 3-round burst that caught the nearest man by surprise, ripping into his side and knocking him back against the car.

As the other two hardmen turned toward Bolan, he saw his backup team moving into place. Shepard and three of his operatives were running down the opposite side of the street with automatic pistols raised.

With them was the wild-bearded Travis Lathrop. The cartel defector had begged for a chance to go against Parker, and Shepard felt he'd earned it. The merc had won his trust, and now he won his chance for payback. And with Shepard's recent losses, it was good to have a professional join the ranks.

Parker sensed Lathrop a moment before the American was on him, his arm outstretched, his automatic pistol pointing at the merc leader's head.

The British hardman turned just as the gun went off. The blast rocketed his head back, and he spun around, falling across the hood of the car.

Lathrop kept firing the automatic, first at the driver, then at the other shotgunner, using speed and surprise to protect himself from a counterattack.

Shepard's people were beside him, unloading volley after volley into the Carib Command gunners.

In only a few seconds the entire team was wiped out.

Two unmarked ISF cars pulled up behind the permanently stalled battle wagon.

Bolan jogged out into the street, jumped into the back seat of one of them, then sat back as the escape cars roared down the suddenly empty street.

16

Bolan parked his Jeep in the paved and walled-in lot of a private club perched on a grassy hillside overlooking the Caribbean. He was parked three slots to the left of one of the familiar Mercedeses from the ISF fleet of armored cars. Colonel Mantrell was already out of his car and walking toward the Executioner.

"I got your message," Bolan said. "What's going on?"

"We'll talk inside," Mantrell replied, grasping the warrior's shoulder and guiding him toward the brightly painted restaurant. "After you."

"Am I pointman again?" Bolan asked.

Mantrell looked surprised.

"Just thinking of the last time we rendezvoused at one of your favorite restaurants."

The ISF colonel laughed. "Tonight your safety is guaranteed. At least inside these doors," he said, leading Bolan through the front of the restaurant.

They passed through a crowd that was composed mostly of elegantly dressed locals and a few well-heeled travelers. Bottles of spring water, chilled wine and rainbow-colored mixed drinks took up a lot of space on the small round tables. Soca music played softly but urgently in the background. The synthesized soul-calypso music filled the room from several strategically placed speakers so that it became a part of the atmosphere.

They took a small table waiting for them in the shadowed alcove at the back of the restaurant, close to the clanking and sizzling sounds of the kitchen, where the chefs were preparing their seafood specialties.

The alcove provided them with a secluded view of the rest of the customers. Bolan's practiced eye picked out a few "couples" who seemed to be a lot more serious than a night out on the town called for. Their low-key conversations took precedence over their food.

The more he studied the "guests" of the club, the more Bolan realized they had the controlled and observant bearing of police or security types. They were all men and women who knew how to blend into a crowd.

Professionals.

"There some kind of convention going on?" Bolan asked.

"You're among friends here. I've assembled them here because we're about to make a sweep through Cape Brethren, rounding up known members of Carib Command. We're also targeting several of the businesses that have been collaborating with the cartel. Thanks to the people we rolled up at the SeaScape, we've got a lot of new leads."

"You need some help?" Bolan asked.

"No," Mantrell replied, looking at the plainclothes troops scattered around the restaurant. "Not for this part of it anyway. But I do have something else in mind."

"Put it on the table and we'll talk about it."

"This raid we're launching will precipitate a counterstrike from Carib Command," Mantrell said. "We're pretty sure it will come from the group of mercs they're keeping in reserve out on Anvil Cay. It's quite a team of specialists."

"I've been briefed on them," Bolan said.

"Our intelligence suggests they are simply waiting for the right time to strike at the seat of government and attempt to install Cambruna. Perhaps when the prime minister is out giving his address to the people."

"And you want me to prevent it?"

"No, I want you to help them launch it."

"It's a bit late to infiltrate their operation," Bolan pointed out. "Especially if they're an outside team brought in just for the job."

Colonel Mantrell shook his head. "I don't want you to infiltrate them. I want you to recruit them."

"What's the offer?"

"Same as they're getting from Cambruna's people. Plus a bonus. They get to keep their lives if you can convince them of the errors of their ways."

Bolan leaned forward on the table as Mantrell spun the scenario the ISF had devised.

Ever since Mantrell first got wind of the mercenaries who were stationed on the remote cay, he'd kept a discreet eye on them. He figured it was better to know where and what the opposition was up to than to wipe them out and risk having another unknown force come into the islands.

"What have they been doing?" Bolan asked.

"Training mostly, keeping in shape."

"How are you keeping tabs on them?"

The colonel smiled. "Two special teams. The first is a unit of naval commandos led by Granville Seward."

"A good man," Bolan said, remembering how the ISF commander performed under fire.

"And then there is a more devious unit that has actually mingled with the mercenaries, eavesdropping on their plans and loosening their tongues."

"A distaff squad?" Bolan probed.

"Exactly," Mantrell said. "Once a week a seaplane ferries in supplies and female companionship to keep the mercenaries in the style they're accustomed to. It picks up their spirits—"

"And you pick up some good intelligence."

"Right. Most of the women come from cartel bordellos, and some of them are willing to talk for the right price. Apparently—in their sober moments—the mercs spend a good deal of their time looking over blueprints for Government House."

"Looks like they're planning on moving in."

"That's the plan," Mantrell agreed. "We're hoping to modify it a bit. You see, the mercs are usually stone drunk from the time the girls arrive to the time they leave."

"Best time to make an approach."

"The seaplane's scheduled to go back there this evening," Mantrell said. "One of *our* pilots will be flying it. The girls will actually be our operatives."

"Those are hard-core mercs," Bolan said. "I'm sure your people are good, but it might be more than they can handle."

"That's why I want you and Granville to go in there at the same time. Handle it whatever way it has to be handled."

THE SEAPLANE LANDED on the calm waters of Anvil Cay, throttling back as it drifted toward the long wooden dock.

Onshore four mercs whooped at the sight of the aircraft, waving their arms and forming a welcoming committee on the dock.

It was always the same. Though two dozen mercs were quartered on the island, only a small crew unloaded the plane and escorted the women onshore. Two men from the crew had already started to party, staggering so badly it was obvious they didn't need anymore liquor supplies from the plane.

Farther inland a handful of other mercs nosed out from the lean-tos and tents pitched near a cluster of hammock-strung palm trees. Despite their kamikaze reputations, none of the mercs looked especially fierce. Their skin was sunburnt, their hair long, and they were dressed in cutoffs and T-shirts.

They'd been living wild, and now that the seaplane arrived they were looking to get wilder.

As soon as the loading crew tied the plane to the dock, a woman with flaming red hair and tight jeans disembarked, stepping onto the pontoon, then jumping onto the dock. The man who caught her grabbed her by the hips and swung her wildly in the air.

But then he set her down gently, standing as still as a statue. "Hands off or head off," she whispered, pressing the barrel of the small automatic under his chin.

The three other men soon found themselves similarly overwhelmed by armed ISF agents as the rest of the women in the war party swarmed over them and led them to shore.

Luther Madden sat in the sand, his callused, scarred hands folded around his shins as he looked out toward the docked seaplane. He was leaning with his back against the trunk of a palm tree that curved over him like a shady street lamp.

Moonlight shone on the water, and moonshine shone in his face, thanks to the steady supply of island spirits from a Cape Brethren rum shop.

Madden was getting an early start on the night's festivities. It was standard procedure for his crew. Train like an SOB night and day, then let off steam at least one night a week.

Like the assassins of old who showed their followers a glimpse of heaven before sending them into battle, he believed in letting them live it up while they could. In this line of work, dying was an occupational hazard.

They'd been here in the Caribbean collecting pay and carrying on long enough. Soon it would be time to pay the piper, as it had in all the African wars he'd fought. Madden's team would lead the life of the idle rich until the time came to fly into some international airport and take over the tower, seize a radio station or carry out a coup with a few well-placed shots. His team would usually stay around just long enough to usher in the new man, then beat it before the new guy decided it was best to liquidate his coconspirators.

It was a rough business but it had its rewards, he thought as he heard sultry laughter sailing in the breeze. A group of women were heading his way, holding their arms around his men.

A few seconds later he saw they were training weapons on his men. It didn't fully register until he pushed himself up from the sand and for the first time noticed the odd expressions on the faces of his troops.

The men had been caught off guard.

"What the hell happened?" he shouted, stepping toward his men. "How did you let them do this?"

Cold metal dug into the back of his neck, just above his shoulders where it could sever his spinal cord.

"Like this," said the man behind him.

Madden turned his head and saw a man in a black wet suit, and behind him were several other men in night-black commando gear. And out in the dark waters he could see shadows knifing toward the shore as several inflatables drove up onto the beach.

He knew how it happened. While the team of sultry-eyed sappers had come in on the seaplane and got the drop on his men, a team of commandos had come in from the sea to wrap things up.

A nice operation, he thought.

A surge of rum-fueled hostility swept through his bloodstream, taking control of him before he could think.

He turned his head to the right to distract the man with the gun on him, then suddenly whipped back to his left, leaning over and planting a back kick straight up to the man's midsection.

But instead of hitting his target, his leg was deflected by a rock-hard forearm sweep.

The Executioner moved by an instinct honed by years of hand-to-hand combat. As soon as Madden turned, the warrior turned also, stepping slightly back out of reach of the chest-crushing back kick.

His arm swept in a circular motion that caught the merc's foot just above the ankle. Then he slammed it down as hard as he could. Madden cried out as one of his leg muscles ripped. His foot came down hard on the sand, stunning him with the impact. Bolan followed through with an inside roundhouse kick, his clenched toes hitting the mercenary like a pickax. He went down with a cracked rib.

Madden managed to stay on his knees, looking back at the black-clad warrior with a death's-head grin, half from pain, half from fury at being caught so cleanly by the other side.

Bolan took one step forward and pressed the barrel of the Beretta in the center of the man's forehead.

All around him the ISF agents were rounding up the hardmen at gunpoint and leading them to the circle where Madden waited for his fate.

"It's time to make a deal, Luther," the Executioner said.

Madden's mood changed instantly, the defiance replaced by curiosity. "What kind of deal?"

"We pay out your contract, and you and your people go to work for us," Bolan said. "Then, when this thing's over, you fly out of here a free man."

"Yeah," Madden agreed, seeing a way out, "yeah, we can do that."

"Just so you understand," Bolan said, raising his voice so everyone could hear, "the deal goes for all of you and it goes against all of you. One guy crosses us, the deal's off—and you all go down."

Madden got to his feet, shrugging off the pain from his rib. "What do you want?"

"Missions and makeup of your teams. Strike teams. Sniper teams. Communications you use with Cambruna. Whatever you've got set up with him, I want to know to the smallest detail."

"What for?" he asked. "You got us. We won't be able to carry any of it out."

"Yeah, you will," Bolan said. "Right down to the last shot."

17

At three o'clock in the afternoon Prime Minister Reardon appeared on the balcony of Cape Brethren's town hall, the historic redbrick building where royal governors, admirals, pirate chieftains and St. Andreas politicians had addressed the people for the past few hundred years.

It was a tradition in the island nation for the leader of the ruling party to take to the streets in times of trouble and show the citizens that he was in control and unafraid, ready to lead them out of it.

It was a tradition that had its dangers, judging by the number of ISF security men in dark suits and dark glasses who stood near the prime minister on the balcony and milled about in the crowded square below him.

The rally had drawn people from all walks of life—shopkeepers and street vendors, Carib Command sympathizers, tourists, reporters, locals and a half-dozen discreetly placed outsiders dressed in faded khakis, standard garb for Luther Madden's mercenaries.

As the rally progressed, sometimes taking on a festive air, other times a sermonlike atmosphere created by the paternal prime minister, the men in khaki drifted into a second-floor apartment above a liquor store owned by a cartel insider.

Carib Command informers watched their move with surreptitious glee, savoring secret knowledge that Prime Minister Reardon was on his way out and their man, Dedrick Cambruna, would soon be in.

"Trouble exists on our island," the prime minister said. "It always has, always will. Life is not always easy on St. Andreas, but it can be lived with honor.

"Unfortunately a certain corrupt element on our island wishes to exploit these troubles for their own benefit, an element led by a poseur named Dedrick Cambruna. He says he wants to end imperialism, to cut off the outsiders he claims are ruining our island with development. Beneath that pose of a patriot is a scoundrel, a man with murder in his heart. A man so power-mad he's trying to take the elected government away from you. In fact—"

The crack of a rifle echoed across the square, almost on cue from the prime minister's words.

A blotch of red appeared on Reardon's shirt.

Another shot rang out, and another bloody patch appeared on his chest. He staggered back across the balcony and dropped into the arms of one of his security men, who quickly pulled him inside.

The crowd fell silent at the shots. Then, as if they were joining in one loud scream, their voices rose in anguish. But many in the crowd were shouting in victory, exulting that Carib Command had finally made its move.

The khaki-clad mercenaries were seen running from the apartment house and losing themselves in a crowd gone wild.

As the people raced from the square, the sound of an ambulance siren drowned out their cries, and soon the blood-covered body of Prime Minister Reardon was seen being carried on a stretcher into the ambulance's wide double doors. Accompanied by unmarked police cars, it roared off toward the hospital in the center of the town.

And the Carib Command watchmen notified their superiors that the target had fallen.

STAGE TWO OF THE ASSAULT began as soon as the sniper fire was heard in the square. Headed by Luther Madden himself, the second team went into action on the other side of the cape, storming the gates of Government House with the rest of his force.

Explosions punctured the seaside quiet with concussive effect, blasts rolling down the shores like manic thunder.

The main gate fell off its hinges; the gate house was riddled with machine-gun fire.

The carport became a battlefield as uniformed guards fell in bloody heaps alongside the mercenaries who breached the entrance, commandeered the elevators, then fanned out through the white-pillared center of power on St. Andreas.

From inside the captured Government House, Madden radioed Cambruna, whose yacht was floating offshore as it had so many days before.

But this day was different.

Today the cartel leader's ship was literally coming in. He stood at the helm of the yacht as the small fleet of Carib Command powerboats headed for shore—and for rule.

There was no opposition at the marina. The boats of the cartel fleet tied up at the docks, then spilled their gunmen onto the shore.

With unhidden exhilaration, Dedrick Cambruna marched through the sundered gates of Government House with his heavily armed supporters beside him.

Everywhere he looked he saw bloody bodies lying on the ground—lying on *his* ground.

By the time he reached the main house itself, he had a score of hard-core supporters walking in step with him. Chief among them was Brigadier General Adam Innis, the former head of the IDF, who'd joined the prime minister's council of advisers a year ago and since then had fed every scrap of inside information he could to Dedrick Cambruna.

Cambruna paused at the head of his troops when they reached the carport. Surveying the carnage accomplished by his imported team of mercenaries, he led the way into the elevators, then brought his inner circle down to the war room, where Luther Madden waited for him.

It appeared that the battle had raged just as heavily down here. Uniformed guards were sprawled across the carpeted corridors, and in the war room itself a number of bodies were scattered on the floor.

Madden stood beside the large desk in the center of the room, a submachine gun at rest in his hands.

"It's all yours, Mr. Cambruna," he announced.

Like an underworld ambassador accepting his seat at the UN, Cambruna nodded toward the mercenary. "Excellent work, Luther," he said, sitting in the seat and gripping the red mahogany surface of the desk. He looked down at his reflection in the well-polished surface and saw the face of a leader looking back at him.

It was a vision he'd waited years to see, a vision he'd helped create. There was a vacuum in St. Andreas, and only he was strong enough to fill it.

"It's over now," he said as he sat back in the soft-cushioned chair.

But then he heard a loud fusillade of automatic fire coming from upstairs. More gunfire sounded from the elevator.

And then he heard an even more dangerous sound.

"It's not over yet," a voice said.

Cambruna was paralyzed with shock for several instants as he looked around the room for the source of the voice. Then he realized it was coming from one of the dead men, a man in black who'd been sprawled on the floor near the wall across from him.

The man got to his feet, despite the gaping bullet holes in his chest.

At the same time several other "corpses" rose from the floor, aiming weapons at Cambruna's men. Colonel Mantrell stood among them.

"A hoax!" Camruna shouted, casting a poisonous look at Luther Madden. "It's a hoax—" Before he finished speaking, he grabbed the subgun from Madden's hand and turned it on the man in black.

It clicked empty. He realized then that the mercenary was part of the hoax.

Cambruna grabbed for his 9 mm Smith & Wesson, but Bolan anticipated his move and brought the 93-R into play, firing a triburst at the would-be dictator of St. Andreas.

The leader of Carib Command clutched at the bullet holes that ran across his chest like bloodred ribbons.

He was still clawing at his automatic pistol as the impacts of the 9 mm rounds carried him back from the desk and knocked him against the wall.

His gaze fell upon the brigadier general, who'd also made a move for his side arm—and paid for it with a bullet to his head, fired from Colonel Mantrell's booming automatic.

The general died instantly, dropping like a rock to the floor. Cambruna fell beside him a few seconds later, his last sight the general's bloodied skull.

MACK BOLAN WALKED across the grounds of Government House, past the site where apparent miracles had taken place. Thanks to the "dirty tricks" squad from Shepard's technical-service division, the dead men were able to rise again, shaking off the effects of fake blood.

Prime Minister Reardon was also part of the miracle, standing larger than life in front of the government mansion as he announced to television reporters that *he* was alive and well, but that the leader of Carib Command couldn't make the same claim.

In the background stood the ISF "mercs" who'd faked the assassination, playing out the roles originally intended for Luther Madden's crew.

Out at sea a flock of helicopters filled the horizon, part of the joint Caribbean-U.S. task force that was landing on St. Andreas at the request of Prime Minister Reardon to help protect the nation from the armed insurrection.

Bolan ducked under the thrumming rotors of an unmarked chopper that had just landed on the lawn in front of Government House, an airborne taxi sent by Hal Brognola.

The Executioner climbed into the cabin and gave a thumbs-up signal to the pilot. His tour in paradise was over.

America is the prime target in a global holocaust

STONY MAN™ 14

DEADLY AGENT

Joseph Ryba is the man who would be king—of a new
Bohemian empire. The Czech official is poised to unleash
a plague that would put Europe at his mercy. Germ warfare
missiles hidden stateside would render the world's watchdog
powerless. Mack Bolan, Able Team and Phoenix Force race
along a tightrope to find and dismantle the deadly arsenal
without forcing Ryba's hand—a situation that would result
in nothing short of global holocaust.

In February, look for a new piece of action
from Gold Eagle...

D. A. HODGMAN

STAKEOUT
SQUAD
LINE OF FIRE

A skyrocketing crime rate forces Miami Chief of Police
John Kearn to create a special police unit. STAKEOUT SQUAD's
objective is to ambush violent criminals at the scene,
sending an unmistakable message to would-be perps.

Don't miss LINE OF FIRE, the first installment of Gold Eagle's
newest action-packed series, STAKEOUT SQUAD!

Look for it in February, wherever Gold Eagle books are sold.

Or order your copy now by sending your name, address, zip or postal code, along
with a check or money order (please do not send cash) for $4.99 for each book
ordered ($5.50 in Canada), plus 75¢ postage and handling ($1.00 in Canada), payable
to Gold Eagle Books, to:

In the U.S.	In Canada
Gold Eagle Books	Gold Eagle Books
3010 Walden Ave.	P. O. Box 636
P. O. Box 9077	Fort Erie, Ontario
Buffalo, NY 14269-9077	L2A 5X3

Please specify book title with order.
Canadian residents add applicable federal and provincial taxes.

SS1

**In the Deathlands, the past and future
clash with frightening force....**

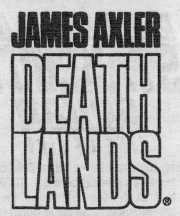

JAMES AXLER

DEATH LANDS®

Trader Redux

Years of struggle in the lawless remnants of humanity have made
Ryan Cawdor a bold and undisputed leader. Yet now, he may have
to contend with his former mentor, the enigmatic Trader, as their
survival skills are tested on a perilous journey down the mighty
Colorado and into the Grand Canyon's mile-deep crags.

Imagine your worst nightmare. It's called Deathlands.